SHELBY'S SECRET

ONCE A MARINE, ALWAYS A MARINE - BOOK 4

KORI DAVID

COKEA, LLC

Shelby's Secret
By: Kori David

This is an original publication of CoKeA, LLC.

This is a work of fiction. Names, characters, places and incidents either are the product of the author's imagination or are used factiously, and any resemblance to actual persons, living or dead, business establishments, events, or locales is entirely coincidental. CoKeA, LLC or the author, does not have any control over and does not assume any responsibility for third-party websites or their content.

www.KoriDavid.com

❀ Created with Vellum

I want to give many thanks to Lt. Lynn Koliboski of the Mesa Police Department for all the help in understanding police procedure when it comes to crime scenes. And for all the times that I just snuck into your office for chats about guns, bad guys, and officer mindset. You've made this book so much better because you care.

To Sgt. Kevin Baggs, of the Mesa Police Homicide Division, thank you so much for making the details of my crime scenes so much more interesting and gory. And for the stories and the steps involved in solving a murder, you will never know how much your time meant to me. Thank you.

There is also a certain, shy, Officer in Internal Affairs of the Mesa Police Department that was gracious enough to let me grill him about what happens when the public makes a complaint or when an officer gets into trouble. He didn't want to be named, but you know who you are and I appreciated all of your wisdom.

And to all my friends in Communications, this book is for you. For every day that you show up to make sure the citizens and our officers are safe, I thank you. The general public will never know how stressful and yet rewarding your job is. Being the first, first responder isn't for everyone and you all do it with grace and style. You're all amazing!

CHAPTER 1

Sergeant Mike Hanson was about dead. More zombie really . . . the walking-barely-talking dead when he got the call.

Another homicide.

The scene was bright, lit by the light bars on the patrol cars. A couple of early-bird reporters trying to make a name for themselves were off to the side, attempting to get a shot of anything interesting and occasionally yelling out a question to the officers passing by. He parked, and Patrol Sergeant Dave Martineau approached his F-250 before he had the door open.

"Hey, Mike. Sorry to get you up again or did you even sleep?"

"Two glorious hours. Whatcha got?"

Dave shook his head. "Not a normal one, that's for damn sure."

They fell in step as Mike headed toward the large warehouse already cordoned off with yellow crime tape. An officer stood on the side of the building, one hand bracing against the brick wall and the other on his hip. Hard to tell in the dark, but it looked like he was heaving his guts up.

"New guy?" Mike asked, pointing toward the officer.

Dave chuckled and nodded. "It's his second week out of academy, and he wanted to see a dead body to prove he could hang with the big boys."

Mike shared a tired laugh. Every time an officer-in-training went to the scene of a homicide one of two things happened—either they ran and puked, or they stayed to gut it out and turned a pearly shade of white. They didn't always pass out, but a good portion of the younger ones ended up face planting anyway.

Turning his attention from the rookie, he noticed most of the seasoned guys looked more disturbed than he would have thought. "You said it's not normal?"

"It's fucking sick," Dave said. "Almost twenty years on the street and I've never seen something like this."

That didn't sound promising. They'd had their share of some fairly gruesome crime but if Dave said the scene was sick, then Mike didn't want to look. He really didn't. Not that he hadn't seen some fucked-up shit over in Iraq during two tours with the Marines, but that was war and to be expected. This was home, and he still didn't get how people could butcher one another the way they did. And for the petty reasons they came up with. "What's the ETA on the medical examiner?"

"Anytime now. I told them they'd need at least two on this one, but I asked for Casey specifically."

"That's good. She's the best. What's the scene like?"

"Staged."

Mike threw a look at his friend. Dave actually looked spooked, and that was odd because the man wasn't squeamish. "Staged how?"

Dave pursed his lips and then shook his head again. "It's something you just have to see."

The smell hit him first. He'd once tried to describe the scent of decomposing flesh in a report and gave up. There just weren't enough words. Or maybe he didn't know the right words. But the stench was a slap to the face and made his eyes water. The fast food burger he'd choked down four hours ago churned.

The warehouse was old construction and had two main areas, split down the middle by a cement wall. Broken roll-up bay doors stood open, as was the single regular-size door occupying the center of the wall. The music playing softly puzzled him. Like a tune he was supposed to know but couldn't quite place. He shot a questioning look at Dave.

He just pointed. "I felt the scene should be kept the way it was, music included."

The music got louder as he continued into the room.

And found himself in Hell.

"Jesus Christ," he muttered, struggling to breathe through his mouth. His stomach flipped more violently this time, and he had to choke down the bile that rose. Mike hadn't had such a visceral reaction to a crime scene in years.

Dave wasn't even bothering to hide his revulsion. He had a handkerchief pressed to his nose and mouth. He was the smart one. "Have you ever seen anything like this?"

Mike was too stunned to answer. The scene before him was like something out of a twisted *Grimm's Fairy Tale*. "Staged" was the word Dave had used. He wasn't kidding. Everything about this scene was placed to elicit a response.

The victim was female—maybe—it was difficult to tell. She was in a turn-of-the-century-style dress with bonnet, hands and feet tied to the ropes of a homemade wood plank swing that hung from the twenty-foot ceiling. Long, kinky, curly, blonde hair held its shape on her head. Probably a wig. Dead flower petals made a carpet beneath her, as if to cushion a fall that the ropes around her wrists and ankles prevented.

Her face was missing.

The skin peeled off—showcasing muscle and tendons and murky white eyeballs that stared sightlessly forward. The image was creepy as fuck.

"Well, this is about the weirdest thing ever," a female voice said from behind.

Mike didn't turn. He'd worked with Casey Henderson on too many cases over the years and instantly recognized her wry tone. She was the spunky kid sister that he'd never had, and they'd hit it off at their first crime scene together. "What do you think the walls are coated with?"

"If I had to guess, I'd say blood. It's overwhelmingly copper smelly in here. From the desiccation of the face, I'd say she was exsanguinated at some point so that's probably the vic's blood." She walked past Mike and pointed at the walls. "And since I just repainted my living room, I can tell you that looks like about a gallon."

"I hope it wasn't red," Mike said.

Casey turned and smiled, seemingly oblivious to the smell and gore. "Nope." And she didn't elaborate.

She never did. The one thing Mike really knew about the senior medical examiner was that she lived for death. She was too young to stare at corpses and scenes like this, but she was a near genius at forensics. She had more degrees than most doctors, and a morbid sense of humor.

Casey talked and dressed like she'd recently escaped from a grunge band. Her short hair was black with streaks of red and blond, and the pierced eyebrow gave her an exotic look that turned more than a couple of heads.

"Oh, are you done puking?" Casey directed the question

over Mike's shoulder with a big false smile plastered on her face and an evil look in her eyes.

Mike turned to see the young officer standing in the door, misery written on his pale greenish face. He nodded and tried to smile back. Mike was proud of the young man. Not a drop of vomit had landed on his uniform.

"Great, I need help gathering up all these fat little maggots."

The poor guy's throat worked, and he turned and ran out of the room—the sound of imminent projectile expulsion of anything left in his body ringing through the empty space.

"That was mean," Mike said. He nodded toward Dave, letting him leave the nasty scene as well. One too many people inside could mess up evidence.

Casey circled the swing, snapping shots of everything she could see and sweeping wide arcs in case the camera could catch something they all missed. "I met him last week while examining that dead homeless guy they found over off of Van Buren. He's all brawn and no brains."

"He hit on you right away?" He walked the scene, pulling on latex gloves as he went and making sure to stay on the outside perimeter of Casey's circle. Casey didn't date cops. But watching the rookie try was always fun.

"Yep, and then acted as if I should be grateful for the attention." She stopped taking photos long enough to roll her eyes. "Is he even old enough to shave, much less carry a gun?"

Mike smiled. Whatever man ended up with the fiery little examiner would have his hands full. "You can't blame the guy, Case. You're gorgeous and smart. It's an intriguing combination."

Hitting the button on the mini boom box shut off the song that was on repeat. He moved to the other side of the room and turned to take it in. He realized Casey was staring.

"Was that an actual compliment?" She wrinkled her nose and turned back to continue taking pictures.

"When you take swabs of blood, make sure to get this spot." Mike pointed to the area on the wall that looked a little darker than the rest.

"Will do. I'll get Lyle to take swabs of everything." she said. "Thanks for shutting off the music. I like Shelby Lynn's music, but the same song over and over gets on your nerves."

"Oh, hell," Mike cursed quietly.

Casey looked up in surprise. "What?"

"Dave said the scene was staged. I thought it was maybe some twisted way of getting a reaction, but it's a different kind of stage."

"What am I missing?" Casey rarely missed anything so she looked annoyed.

"You don't watch music videos, do you?"

Casey shrugged. "It's not like anyone actually *plays* videos anymore. All that's on is that reality-show crap teenagers binge watch, and I don't have time to sit around on YouTube all day."

An uneasy feeling crept up Mike's spine, raising the hair on the back of his neck. "This scene is out of Shelby Lynn's first music video. Back when they did show music videos. But what's the message? Or is this a threat?"

"Oh shit. Isn't she coming to town soon for a concert?"

Mike nodded, the whole scene before him taking on a new and even more sinister meaning. "Her last concert stop for this tour. She's playing three nights."

"How do you know all that?"

"My friends' wives love her music and all have tickets to go. The concert is all they've talked about for months now."

"Then let's hope this is just some sick fan art, and doesn't mean anything else."

Mike moved closer to the woman in the swing. She was

small but full figured, and with the wig on, she could be Shelby Lynn's body double. But something was wrong with the face. Otherwise, why remove it?

~

SHELBY LYNN COLLINS was physically exhausted, but also stuck in the vortex known as insomnia. She hadn't slept in more than twenty-four hours. Thank God for make-up artists because she had an interview in roughly five hours, and she looked like road kill.

It had been a long drive from the concert in Austin, Texas, to her home town of Phoenix, Arizona. And, being home was great. She was a desert rat deep down, and the heat of the summer night sunk into her bones in a good way. Her manager had rented a luxury mansion on Camelback Mountain, giving Shelby a view of the city at night that few could afford but no one should miss.

The hour was a couple of minutes past four a.m. and the night was quiet as Shelby relaxed on the patio.

The ping of an incoming email from the open laptop on the patio table intruded. She almost didn't look at it, but she was up, and the message might be something important like a schedule change. Not that her manager wouldn't handle the issue. The woman was militant in her efficiency.

She opened the email, belatedly realizing she probably shouldn't have since she didn't recognize the address and no subject line existed. But she was tired, and her finger got click-happy.

Her very first song started to play from the speakers. Then her lyrics crawled up the right side as the music played, and the screen wasn't blank any longer. It was filled with a likeness of her video.

Shelby's hand froze over the keyboard as the screen turned from black to something else.

The camera was hand-held, and it wiggled and bounced as the person filming moved. The subject matter caused the instant horror. Shelby hoped to God it was a sick joke. Maybe some kind of prank by a budding special effects student. Because if the woman in the swing was real, then she was dead and it looked like blood dripped from the walls.

"What in the hell are you doing up? You're supposed to be sleeping." Margaret 'Madge' Henner's stern voice cut into the night like a sonic boom and made Shelby jump so violently she almost fell out of her chair.

"Jesus," Shelby said, her hand flying up to her chest to keep her heart from beating right out of her rib cage.

"What's wrong?" Madge asked. Her brow furrowed as she waited for Shelby to speak.

But she couldn't.

The fist-sized lump of dread had lodged in her throat, and all she could do was point. Point to the screen that had paused, cutting off the song, but leaving a close-up of the poor woman's mutilated face.

Actually, not even a face was left. It had been peeled off, leaving something straight out of a horror flick, staring sightlessly into the now-still camera.

Madge wasn't a small or petite woman, in fact she could have easily played football professionally. Wide, thick shoulders tapered to a trim waist kept in shape by clean eating and a workout regimen that professional athletics would have a hard time completing. But when she came around the table and played the video again, she turned into the fussy mother hen Shelby had first met all those years ago in Nashville.

Those long arms wrapped around her from behind, and Madge hugged her hard, while simultaneously slamming the laptop closed. "That was sick."

8

"Was that real?" Shelby hoped that it wasn't, even if the hope was naive.

"I don't know, but if it was—"

"We should call the police," Shelby said.

Madge nodded. "Maybe they'll be able to do something or maybe not. We don't even know where that is."

Shelby stood on shaky legs. She held the edge of the table until she was reasonable sure she wouldn't collapse in a heap. It was a good thing she hadn't been hungry for dinner, the way her stomach churned. "I'll make the call."

"Go lay down. I'll make the call."

"Won't they need to speak to me, since the email was sent to my account?"

Madge shrugged. "Possibly. But no one will rush right out to see an email, no matter what I tell them is on it."

"Who would do that?"

"Who knows, but I'm hiring more security."

Shelby shook her head. "We have enough, Madge. I already feel like I'm living in a prison. Just tell the guys to be especially vigilant."

"Was there anything else with this email?"

"That was it. I was so tired I didn't even think, just opened it and—you saw the rest."

Madge grabbed the laptop and ushered Shelby inside the cool interior.

Suddenly, the glass walls facing Phoenix didn't seem as wonderful as they had when she'd first seen them. Now she felt vulnerable. Exposed in a way that she hadn't before. She'd done TV, sold-out stadiums, award shows—you name it. But with one email she was stripped naked with no protection around her at all. "And cancel that interview today. I want to be here and available if the police need to speak to me."

"Will do. And, Shelby?"

Shelby had already turned toward her wing of the behemoth home, but she looked back over her shoulder at her manager. "Yeah?"

"Actually sleep this time."

She tried to smile but by the look on Madge's face the gesture probably looked scary. Madge didn't have to worry, Shelby was suddenly so tired she couldn't keep her eyes open. Maybe if she went to sleep, she'd wake up with perspective. In the cold light of day, the email wouldn't be what it looked like. The message would be some bad prank and not a dead woman dressed up to look like her.

With no face.

CHAPTER 2

"Goddamn it. How did this get out so fast?" Mike threw a copy of the *Arizona Republic* across the room. The newspaper made an unsatisfying rustle as it sailed into the wall opposite his desk.

He didn't expect an answer as he vented about the age-old problem of leaks in the department. They'd been burned before when a vital piece of an investigation got leaked and their case went to shit, and someone else had died. The details had been kept out of the news for two whole days before this story.

Detective Daniel Wolfe sat in the only other chair in the office, drinking coffee and wisely staying silent during the brief, but loud, moment of frustration. Wolfe was new to homicide, two weeks to be exact, having come over from burglary. Mike had assigned Wolfe to work the case with him. Daniel was thorough and got in his paperwork on time. Plus he'd had a very good streak of arrests during his time in burglary. This would be his first homicide.

"I read the story this morning. Whoever their "source at the department" is gave them pretty much everything except the fact the victim was a replica of that country star's video. Shelly Lynn?"

"Shelby Lynn."

"Maybe those reporters don't listen to country music and didn't make the connection."

"Let's hope they don't. Where are you on the faceless vic?" Mike asked.

"No I.D. yet, and her prints aren't on file."

That didn't mean much other than their victim hadn't held any sort of government job, and she didn't have a record. Mike just hoped it wasn't a dead end.

"I checked with missing persons to see if they had any females on their list that matched a general description of our vic," Daniel said. "They'll get back to me later today."

"I'm just waiting on a call from Casey about the autopsy," Mike said.

Wolfe looked down into his coffee.

Mike knew he wasn't thrilled about viewing the autopsy, but he'd done well at the warehouse. Everyone had left and Mike wanted to get Daniel's initial thoughts. He'd turned an interesting shade of green, but he hadn't lost his dinner and focused on the details, not the smell. Of course, his new detective had been a Marine once upon a time, so in Mike's eyes, he was upholding a gold standard of performance by not blowing chunks all over the crime scene.

He didn't go around Semper Fi'ing, but he and Wolfe had a bond and they both knew it. Being a Marine was a brotherhood, and it always would be.

"I'll be ready when the call comes in. In the meantime, I'll work on canvassing the area again for any homeless that might have seen something that night."

"Great. Also, start calling around to the wig shops. One of the lab techs called and said it's real human hair, so the wig's expensive. Maybe we'll get lucky, and a shop owner will remember selling one recently."

Wolfe nodded. "I'll get right on that." He stood and turned toward the door just as the phone rang.

"Hanson," Mike answered and waved off Wolfe.

"Hey, Mike, this is Amanda in Admin. The Chief needs to see you."

"What time?"

"ASAP is what he said."

Mike felt an eye roll coming on. "I'll be there as quickly as I can."

"I'll tell him."

The line disconnected, and Mike flexed his shoulders. If the issue was about the damn story in the newspaper then Chief Howard would have to yell at someone else. No one in his department was dumb enough to leak info, and he could personally guarantee it. His people knew their lives wouldn't be worth living if he found out they'd been talking to anyone.

He finished his report before heading to the Chief's office. Amanda was on the phone. She smiled and waved him on.

Steven Howard had steadily moved up through the department over the last twenty years. This year would mark his third as Chief of Police. In general, he was a good guy and a good leader, even if Mike thought he kissed the City Manager's ass a bit too much. He'd developed a taste for expensive cigars along the way, so the office held a lingering smell.

"Glad you came, Mike. I have a problem."

"What can I do for you?" One thing he'd learned in both the Marine Corps and in police work—play dumb until you knew what the conversation was about. A copy of the paper sat on the desk between them.

"Seems the press has access to details about the case."

Mike shrugged. "They usually manage it somehow."

"I'd like to find out who's been talking," he said, waving Mike to one of the empty chairs.

The Chief wasn't a yeller. His tone was conversational, almost as if they were co-conspirators as he looked over his polished wooden desk. Sitting forward, forearms resting on either side of the paper, he had an earnest look on his face that said, "If you tell me, we'll be heroes together." Mike admired the tactic, having used it himself a time or two. "I'd like to find out myself. This only makes my job harder." He sat and didn't say anything more.

"You have some new people over in homicide. Anyone you're worried about?"

"Nope." Mike sat back in his chair, totally relaxed. This was a waste of time, and they both knew it. Whatever was on the Chief's mind, he wasn't quite ready to share it.

"I have a meeting in five minutes with the Mayor. I'd like you to come with me."

Now that was a surprise and faster than he'd expected the man to get to the point. "What's it about?" Mike hated walking into something he wasn't prepared for.

"It's a public relations thing, but it involves your case, so I'd like you there to consult."

"You know we can't discuss an open case." Mike kept his face blank, especially since he'd just been quietly reamed about the leak in the paper.

The Chief was a very adept political player. Why he'd need a lowly Sergeant to consult was beyond him, but he'd go. He had political aspirations of his own, at least as far as making Chief himself at some point.

"There might be new information, but the person involved is high profile." He glanced at his gold Rolex. Another expensive habit he'd picked up since promoting to

14

the top office. "And they should be in the conference room now."

Mike rose from his chair and followed his boss out. They rode the elevator down two levels to the large conference room. And Mike wondered who in hell could be important enough to warrant the Mayor's and the Chief of Police's presence just to gather some new info.

SHELBY SAT in a plush chair in the middle of the long table that could easily fit twenty people. The main station of the Phoenix police department was not the most attractive building, but this conference room made up for the utilitarian structure. Madge stood against the far wall, posture ramrod straight and disapproval written across her face. She didn't want Shelby out of the house and away from her security team. Shelby figured enough cops were in the building to mitigate any stress.

"We just want your homecoming to be special," the Mayor said. Again. As if he needed to keep saying it to prove the statement was true. He was a sweet man, who'd made her feel welcome and comfortable. In his fifties, John Nesbit was classically good looking with just a hint of gray at the temples of his blond hair.

He'd been the one to call this meeting with the Chief of Police. Why he was involved wasn't a mystery. She packed stadiums for her concerts and the revenue her three concerts would bring in was good business. After all, if those concerts didn't happen, then millions of dollars in hotels, food, concert tickets and general spending in the great city of Phoenix would be lost.

The door opened, and the energy in the room changed. The first man through was tall, with a severe haircut and a mustache that looked straight out of a seventies porn flick. Not that she'd ever seen one herself, but Madge was fond of pointing out said mustaches—and this one fit the bill. And where Madge got her info, Shelby didn't *ever* want to know.

The man immediately met the Mayor in the middle of the room to shake hands.

What they said was lost on Shelby the moment the second man entered the room. He looked like a thug.

The white, button-up, long-sleeve shirt just made his skin look darker and his shoulders wider. His hair was raven black and contrasted with hazel eyes that were a true hazel and changed color with his mood.

He wasn't a conventionally handsome man. His features were too rough for what society deemed good looking, plus his nose had clearly been broken a couple of times. But what he did as he gave her a quick once-over should've been illegal. Those eyes had started out a lighter green, but the longer they stayed on her, the darker they got.

And when he made love—they'd turn emerald.

She knew from experience.

"Shelby Lynn," he said in the sudden silence.

His tone was faintly mocking and his face seemed made of stone, but only she heard the thread of humor. He'd been the one to suggest using her first and middle name only as her stage name. That had been more than fifteen years ago. When they'd been teenagers.

"Mike." Not Michael, and if anyone called him Mikey, they got their arm broken. Just Mike. Simple and plain. Unlike the man, who was anything but simple. Or plain.

"Glad you remembered," he said. Then he took up a position in the corner, back to the wall, facing the door, keeping everyone in view.

Three pairs of eyes focused on her, and she was glad she'd stopped blushing years ago. Madge's eyebrows were up in her hairline, and Shelby could tell she wanted to know what the hell had just happened, but would wait until they were alone. Small reprieve. The Mayor and the Chief merely looked quizzical.

"You know each other?" This question was from the Mayor.

"Ancient history," Mike answered.

Shelby couldn't help the small stab that comment, and the dispassionate tone, caused. But she smiled at the Mayor, turned up the wattage, and said, "A lifetime ago."

The Chief cleared his throat and stuck out his hand to introduce himself while the Mayor took a seat. "Thank you for coming in, Ms. Collins. I can imagine your schedule is very busy, but we appreciate any light you can shed on this tragedy. Sergeant Mike Hanson is my lead homicide detective on the case. I'm sure he'll have some questions as well."

"He can question us both," Madge said. Her arms were crossed but she'd moved to stand directly behind Shelby's chair. "I saw the email as well." She threw a folded section of the newspaper on the gleaming conference table, all of them watching it slide toward Mike. "That story is what made Shelby determined to come in and talk about the email she received."

"We want to help," Shelby said, quietly. Madge was a mother hen in action.

"Tell me about the email," Mike said.

His gaze caught and held her. Something in her chest squeezed tight, because she hadn't really ever expected to see him again. He was right—they were ancient history, and she needed to act like it. So she made her tone brisk as she described what happened two days prior. The email with the song, the dead woman in the swing, and the parallel to her very first video. She described what she could remember.

Madge filled in the details.

Shelby was proud of the fact her voice stayed even. She couldn't be completely unemotional, because she wasn't; it was too sad and too scary to pretend otherwise.

"Why did you wait two days to report this?"

Shelby looked up at her manager.

"She wanted to call that morning." Madge answered. "I sent her to bed because she hadn't slept, and I went to look at the email again, to make sure it was what we thought it was." She sighed and finally took a seat next to Shelby. "But it was gone."

"What do you mean it was gone?" Mike asked.

"Just what I said. The email just wasn't there. I have a friend who works I.T., and he said the email probably came with a sub-program that erased it within minutes of viewing."

"So you decided not to call police."

Shelby piped up. "I made that decision when Madge told me what happened." She shrugged. "If Madge hadn't seen it herself, I would have thought I'd just imagined it. I'd been without sleep for more than twenty-four hours at that point. My mind could have been playing tricks on me."

"Besides," her manager said, "it's not the first time, or the last time, someone will email or send something weird to Shelby. She's an international superstar. It could have been a sick prank. Why waste your time?"

Shelby glanced at Mike's expression, but he wasn't giving much away. They'd all heard the pride in Madge's voice.

"I'm sure you felt you did the right thing," the Mayor said.

The Chief stayed quiet—merely listening.

Shelby fought the urge to squirm or chatter because the she felt awkward. She should have pushed for this meeting after the email, she knew it. But she hadn't. "When I read the paper this morning, I could no longer convince myself it was just a sick prank. I'm so sorry if I've messed up the investigation." She made eye contact with all three men—two nodded and one cocked his head to the side.

"What else happened?" Mike asked.

How the hell did he know? He couldn't read her the way he used to. Could he? Too much time had passed, and she certainly couldn't read anything in his enigmatic face. That pissed her off a little.

She crossed her arms. It wasn't a defensive move, there was a chill in the room. After all, she was there trying to help.

"How could you possibly know there's something else?"

That question was from Madge, but Shelby couldn't shake the feeling Mike knew her secrets. Which was silly. No one did.

She nodded at Madge who pulled a large plastic bag out of her purse. Sealed within was a folded letter.

"I'm afraid I touched it before I realized what it was," Shelby said.

"I'll need your prints to match them up with the ones on the letter." Mike never moved to touch the package himself. "Tell me what it says."

"They're song lyrics," she said. He was so business-like that it made her feel awkward. As if she were in trouble.

"From a new song that Shelby has been working on," Madge added.

Shelby nodded. "No one has heard it but Madge." She uncrossed her arms, resisting running her hands through her hair. It was a nervous tick and one she'd worked long and hard to eradicate because she was a public figure. The gesture didn't look good in front of her fans or the paparazzi because it betrayed the fact that she was less than composed. "The last time I even worked on it was at my home in Tennessee."

"So, you think this is a stalker?" Mike asked.

"I don't know what to think. I've dealt with everything from hate mail to having both male and female stalkers before, but the letters and appearances have been virtually harmless. Nothing like this has ever happened."

"How was it delivered?"

This time Shelby couldn't stop the small shiver. It was scary to think how close to home it was. "The envelope was slipped into my hairdresser's purse while she was shopping." Mike never shifted his gaze from her. She hugged her arms, unnerved.

"And where was she shopping, Shelby?"

"Three miles from the home we rented."

"You can rest assured, Ms. Collins, we *will* find who did this and make sure it doesn't happen again," The Chief said.

His tone was firm and confident, and Shelby turned to smile at him, relieved to break the intense eye contact with Mike. "I appreciate that, very much. As does my staff."

"Why don't I take Ms. Collins down and scan her prints?" Mike said, as he moved away from the wall.

Madge started to stand, but Shelby put her hand on her thigh under the table to stop her. She wanted a moment alone with the man now standing in front of her. Madge shot her a look, which Shelby ignored, but stayed in her seat.

"Good idea," the Mayor said enthusiastically. "I'll have to be off before you get back, Ms. Collins, but if either of you need anything, please call my office."

She nodded and followed Mike out into the hallway. The walk to the elevator was silent and continued that way to the basement. She found herself in a small room with a new machine that was waist high and looked a bit like a futuristic scanner. The days of an ink pad and roller were apparently over at the Phoenix Police Department. She turned to say something to the big quiet man behind her, but the glittering look in his eyes stopped her. He'd lost the poker face and what she saw was anger. The slow-build kind that lashed out from his expression.

"You left without ever saying goodbye," he said.

His voice was soft, but she still flinched. "I didn't think there was anything more to say," Shelby replied. Her heart accelerated, like a small animal in the presence of a hunter. "We wanted different things, and neither of us was willing to bend."

"I might have compromised. Eventually."

Shelby shook her head. "Not back then. You had a path laid out and come hell or high water, you were following it. I had that same determination. What could I have said that would've changed your mind?"

"I guess there wasn't anything. But I deserved more than an empty room and no note." He reached for her and spanned his hands around her much-smaller waist. "You didn't even kiss me goodbye."

And then his lips were on hers.

CHAPTER 3

*M*ike had meant the kiss to punish. To somehow prove that he'd gotten over her fifteen years ago when she'd walked out on him. But the moment his lips touched her soft pink ones, he couldn't be that guy. Couldn't use what they had to hurt her that way.

He'd walked into that conference room and been blindsided. Those cobalt blue eyes were the same, never done justice in her videos. The over-the-top curly ash blond hair that refused to straighten no matter what she did was the same. It was a little longer and highlighted, but still baby soft.

He'd felt her presence like a punch in the gut. That he'd been able to speak at all was a miracle, much less carry on an intelligent conversation. As it was, he probably sounded like the surly thug he knew he looked like.

All that faded as she responded slowly to his kiss. Her hands slid up his arms but stayed on his biceps. He'd crushed her body against his much-harder one, and she still fit perfectly against him. As if she was made for him. But she wasn't just for him.

And that truth was like a cold splash of water.

The heat of the moment faded, and he pulled back. Her lips were shiny and kiss swollen, but her make-up and hair remained perfect. Like her life away from him. "Well, I've had my goodbye kiss. Now let's get your fingerprints taken," he muttered.

He gave Shelby a lot of credit. She never reacted to anything the way he thought she would, and that kiss was no different. No yelling, no recriminations, no cutting words flung at him for stealing something that millions of men the world over fantasized about.

"You certainly haven't lost your touch. Guess the Marine Corps didn't change everything."

If she was bitter, her light chuckle didn't show it. "That was unprofessional. I won't apologize."

This time her laugh was genuine and hearty. "You never have before, why start now?"

He put the kiss and their past behind him, where it should have stayed and slipped back into cop mode—better than left-behind-former-lover. That was a role he'd never be in again. Shelby had made sure of that. Contrary to what just happened, he was a professional. "Do you have any idea who might want to hurt you?" He asked it while he began setting up the machine for her prints.

She seemed to accept the change in atmosphere as if nothing had happened. "I really don't. In the past, I've had to get a couple of restraining orders. One against an overzealous fan club president and the other against a band roadie, but those were pretty mild cases of stalking. Like Madge said, I've had hate mail and crazy threats, but no one around me seems likely, and they've all had thorough background checks."

"Sounds like your manager is very competent. I assume you have a security detail?"

Shelby nodded and looked up at him.

He didn't want to touch her again, even to take her prints. He was honest enough with himself to know he might not stay detached. But he gritted his teeth and reached for her hand, placing it firmly on the scanner.

"It's a three-man team from a company that came highly recommended in Nashville. They've worked with other singers in similar situations."

"Since I haven't heard of any other singers who've inspired this kind of rage, make sure your team leader gets into contact with me. There are some things they should watch for."

She was quiet for a while as he scanned both hands, her head was down so he couldn't see her face. He wished he could see her expression. Was she terrified, or was this just normal for her business? And he didn't like that he couldn't stay objective. He was about to ask something else about her security but she spoke first.

"Did you ever get married?"

The question was out of the blue. Or maybe it wasn't. Her life as a tabloid princess was there for everyone to see. She'd gotten engaged once, about five years ago, but for whatever reason the wedding hadn't happened. "No."

"Why not?" She took her hand off the scanner and folded them together in front of her. "It was your dream."

Mike went through the door and waved Shelby toward the elevator. Marriage was still his dream, somewhere inside of him. A woman he could love, who would love and understand him. He thought he'd put that aside years ago and then he'd watched his friends begin to fall like dominoes. Each and every one of them had found what Mike only dreamed existed between a man and a woman. And that dark place inside of him had flickered to life.

It was hope.

And then he'd walked into that damned conference room

and seen Shelby. She'd been his hope, his dream. But fame and fortune had been hers. Not a quiet life with a simple man who had simple needs.

He stayed quiet all the way to the elevator. After pressing the button, he pulled out his card holder and a pen. He produced a business card from his pocket, wrote his personal cell number on the back and handed it to Shelby. "If anything else happens, this is my work number. My cell is on the back."

She took the card slowly, her blue eyes wide at his cold tone. "I'm sorry. I shouldn't be asking any personal questions. I guess I was just curious about an old friend."

The ride back up to the conference room was frosty and awkward. As the doors opened, he could see her worried manager standing with the Chief. He motioned Shelby off but stayed behind. "I didn't marry, Shelby, because my dream packed her suitcase fifteen years ago and never looked back."

HE SAT in a beige four-door sedan, half a block away from the Phoenix Police station. He'd chosen the car expressly because there were a million others just like it—everywhere. It was invisible.

Just like he was.

But not to her. She was finally seeing him. He didn't think she understood his message, but she would.

And there she was. Walking out of the glass doors with her huge manager. *Shelby Lynn.* Even her name sounded deli-cate. Her voice might be broadcast for everyone, but her songs were only for him. He'd been her secret love since she started singing, and she wrote her love songs about them being together one day—he was sure of it.

She'll never love you. Why would she?

"Yes, she will," he whined. He gave himself a sharp slap to the forehead. "She already does." Three more sharp quick slaps, and he felt under control again.

Control was important.

Just a glimpse of his love was enough. For now. She was so beautiful and petite, like a doll. Light blond hair that was corkscrew curly. The style was natural and she'd never tried to straighten it. He thought she understood that he preferred her that way. All that make-up they made her wear for the TV performances could be forgiven, because he understood she was sending her messages to him.

She loved him.

Only him.

But she doesn't, you little turd. She sings for everyone else but not you. She doesn't see you.

"But she does."

She could, the voice whispered. *You showed her what we can do. You showed her that we've been watching. All these years.*

"I showed her. I showed her how her first song was about us. About how much our love means to her."

Now you need to show her more. She needs to understand what we are to her.

"Yes." He nodded. The voice was making sense again. Not belittling him like it usually did. Shelby was what was important, and controlling the mean voice that told him he wasn't good enough. The voice that sounded so much like . . . he didn't want to think about *him.*

He gave himself a quick slap to the side of the head, just to make sure he was still in control. The sting was small compared to what might happen if the voice took over. Then it would make him do things. Worse than he'd already done. Things that made his reflection in the mirror all dark and hazy, like he wasn't even there. Just the voice.

But he was back in control.

And he had work to do.

He whistled as he pulled away from the curb. Just another tan car in a desert landscape.

"WANT to tell me what that was back there?"

Shelby pulled her gaze from the odd mix of new businesses and abandoned warehouses that populated downtown Phoenix. Expensive cars mixed with the homeless on Seventh Avenue as they headed away from the police headquarters and back to the mansion on the Camelback Mountain. "I did grow up here, Madge. It was inevitable that I'd run into someone I knew. Eventually." She just hadn't counted on that person being big, muscled and pissed off.

"Tell me about Detective Mike Hanson. He couldn't keep his eyes off you," she said.

"You tell me all the time that men can't keep their eyes off of me," Shelby said. Her tone was dismissive, even though the long looks made her uncomfortable. But she'd learned to deal with it. The constant presence of fans was something they never told you about when you became lucky enough to reach stardom. The stares. Eyes watching everything she did, undressing her, envying her, assessing her—sometimes finding flaws and other times simply adoring.

"Don't play possum with me, young lady. His eyes said all kinds of things, and none of it was the normal stuff you've dealt with."

Shelby sighed. "He loved me once. More than life, he'd said." She could feel moisture welling up in her eyes, and that response ticked her off because there wasn't a damn thing she could do about the situation. Looking away from her manager, she blinked rapidly to keep the tears from falling. Oh sure, she'd laughed it off back in the little room, but when he'd walked into that room with the Chief—well, she'd been glad she was sitting.

"We can talk about it later, honey. But I want to know about him, especially if he's working the case." Madge took one of Shelby's hands and squeezed.

Honestly, the woman was more like a second mother, especially since she'd lost her own at a young age. "Thanks for understanding," she choked out. One lone tear broke loose and scalded a path down her cheek. He'd looked even better than she remembered. He was still huge, especially in the shoulders, and his hair was still black as night. Not a single gray hair yet to mar the shine. And those green eyes of his. Like a forest just before the dawn, deep and mysterious. All courtesy of a fiery Italian mother.

He wasn't magazine pretty, but his rugged features blended together, making him look like some ancient king who battled alongside his men and not from a throne. He'd always made her heart flutter just with a look.

And those lips. Dear God. They were still as magical as she remembered in her dreams. She knew he'd meant the kiss as a punishment, as a final goodbye of sorts, but she didn't think it turned out the way he'd intended. God knows it hadn't for her. She'd been prepared for an assault when he'd pulled her closer, and maybe she felt like she deserved it. But that's not what happened. His lips had touched hers, and a fiery heat ignited low in her, from a place long grown cold.

She sighed. She hadn't thought seeing Mike would be a reality, but she'd harbored a secret yearning. Leaning her head against the warm glass of the window, she stared sightlessly now, lost in the past. Lost to a time when life was rough, but she'd been young and in love with a bad boy. A boy who'd loved her more than she'd loved him, she realized now. She'd been selfish. She hadn't understood that her dreams would crush his.

As a woman, she knew her choices had consequences and coming home would be much harder than she'd thought. She shook her head and admonished herself for being a silly girl.

She was here, and the past was just that. Past. Time to build her future, and nothing and no one was going to stop her.

CHAPTER 4

a noise penetrated the quiet. An urgent chirp that didn't make sense at first. And when it did, Mike reached over and grabbed the offending noise maker. His cell phone. He didn't even bother opening his eyes, knowing it was the middle of the night.

Hitting the on button with his thumb, he held it up to his ear, ready to chew someone's ass for waking him. "Hanson."

"Mike," she whispered. "I'm so sorry to wake you."

"Shelby?" Just like that he was awake. His eyes popped open in the semi dark of his room, and he sat up. Her voice quivered, and her breath came in rapid spurts causing his grip to tighten on the phone. "What's wrong?"

"He did it again."

"Who did what?"

"He murdered another woman."

Mike was already off the bed and had one leg into a pair of jeans that he'd left on the floor.

"And it looks like my third video." She started crying.

The sound knifed through him, but he pushed through

the pain so that he could focus. Get to her. "Did you get another email?"

"Yes," she sobbed. "It's horrible. Can you come over, please?"

"I'll be right there. Don't touch anything, hopefully it won't delete this time."

"It already did."

Mike paused on his way to the door and closed his eyes. "Damn." He heard some sniffs and a deep breath. She was getting herself under control while they talked.

"I recorded some of it on my phone when I realized what it was. Is that okay?"

Mike was glad she sounded stronger. And what she'd done was brilliant. "That's amazing, Shel. I'm out the door now. Make sure your guards know I'm coming. Tell them to look for a black Ford F-250 truck."

"Thank you, Mike."

Once the line disconnected, he grabbed a clean shirt and raked his fingers through his hair. Shoes, keys, notepad, his gun and he was out the door.

The time was exactly one a.m. Once he was in his truck, he placed a call to his lead detective.

"Wolfe."

"Our boy killed again," Mike said. "Shelby Lynn just got another email."

"Shit."

There was a pause, and Mike could hear fabric rustling in the background.

"That's two in less than a week. Same M.O.?"

"I'm on my way to Shelby's now. The bastard's email deleted itself again, but Shelby recorded some of it on her phone."

"Someone was using her head."

The tone was admiring, and Mike had to agree. Not many

folks could think under pressure, especially when the situation involved something gruesome. Like a murder. Seasoned cops wouldn't have reacted so fast. He was damned proud of her, and he'd tell her so when he got there.

"As soon as I get it, I'll forward it to you. I want a hard copy ASAP that we can give to Casey as well. Also check with dispatch, see if they've had questionable or suspicious calls that are holding around abandoned buildings. I want anything, especially noise complaints. Shelby said the scene looked like her third video, and if that's the case, this guy will need another big space."

"Got it. I'll be at the office, waiting."

"Thanks, Daniel."

He hung up and focused on getting to her. The streets were relatively empty this time in the morning, so he quickly reached the freeway and punched it. He took fifteen minutes to get to Shelby from the moment she called.

Her place was something he'd seen only in magazines. The grounds were gated and private, with a long driveway. A guard met him at the gate, flashlight in hand. Mike held up his badge, and the guard nodded and waved him through. He was a big guy, but young. Mid-twenties at the most, but he looked awake and confident. And that's what Shelby needed.

He parked and was met at the door by the manager. She was almost as tall as Mike, and built like she could have competed in the Olympics for power lifting. But the slight sheen around her eyes told the story. She was scared. "Ms. Henner," he greeted.

"Call me Madge, Detective. I have a feeling we'll be seeing a lot of each other. Unless, you catch this guy soon."

Mike nodded. "Madge. Call me Mike, and I will catch him." She looked hard into his eyes, as if gauging the truthfulness in his statement. Whatever she saw there must have assured her.

She nodded and opened the door wide to admit him. "I looked you up, you know," she said as she led the way through the massive foyer.

Imported tiles lined the floor and marble columns flanked an enormous staircase. He could have fit his entire department inside the living room. "I figured you might. Shelby mentioned all the staff had background checks. I assumed that was done by you." And in truth, he didn't mind. He'd never had anything to hide. And he was glad someone was looking out for Shelby. Someone needed to.

"Your mother lives in New York, and your father is deceased. I found a sealed juvenile record. And then an exemplary military career with several medals awarded. Including a Medal of Honor and a Silver Star. Isn't that for combat valor?"

Mike nodded. "It is." But didn't say anything else. He had a feeling she wasn't done.

"I couldn't find out exactly what you did in the Marines, but you finished as a Major. The lack of information leads me to believe you were in Intelligence. You served two tours in Afghanistan, and then came home and immediately went through the police academy. You didn't stay long in patrol, working your way up to sergeant and then moving into homicide, where you've stayed."

"You've done some homework."

"I don't want anyone around Shelby who can't be trusted. She tends to trust a bit too easily for my peace of mind, and I won't have her taken advantage of."

The woman in front of him was a veritable dragon lady, but he could hear the love ringing in her voice. Shelby could inspire that kind of emotion, which is how she became one of the youngest Entertainers of the Year at the Country Music Awards. Two years in a row. "I will catch this guy."

"Before he escalates and hurts her?"

Madge was stopped in front of what looked like an office. French doors were closed, and Mike could see Shelby in the dim room. She was huddled under a blanket, wedged into the corner of a brown leather couch. She faced a gorgeous view of the city and wasn't aware he and Madge were just outside the doors. "I don't lose. Ever."

"I hope so, because Shelby has more than her life at stake here."

Then she moved away before he could question that statement. He opened the door and went inside. The large glass windows showed his approach. He saw her gaze meet his in the reflection.

"Did Madge give you the third degree?" she asked.

Mike smiled a bit grimly. "She just let me know that she'd looked into my background."

"She's a bit of a steamroller, but she has my best interests at heart. She always has."

"Did you read it?" He was genuinely curious if she'd wondered enough to look.

Shelby shook her head. "Madge rattled off the highlights, but looking into your life that way isn't fair."

"The way the entertainment field looks into yours?"

She raised her eyebrows slightly.

The look in her eyes was more innocent than he could believe, considering that she was a world famous singer.

Then she slowly nodded. "I'm not sure how I feel about you reading me that easily, even after all these years. You were doing that back at the station, too."

"It's not really reading you, Shel. Anyone not living under a rock has been bombarded with your life, your success, and your love life. You've been on the covers of magazines and splashed all over TV for years now."

She rolled her eyes. "What love life?"

"You were engaged—what was it—five years ago?"

She snorted. Probably the most unladylike thing she'd done since becoming a superstar. The sound made Mike grin. It was such a normal little thing, something she used to do when they were younger.

"That was a train wreck from the beginning, and I never actually told the jerk I'd marry him."

Mike half sat on the plush arm of the couch, at the other end from Shelby, who was still curled up in the corner. She hadn't moved an inch since they started talking. She was holding a little too still. Her eyes were red and puffy from crying, but her gaze was clear and steady. And she looked amazing. No make-up on, hair in a haphazard bun—she was stunning. "Well, his career took off for about six months after the story broke."

"And that's what the ass was after all along anyway. I was just a means to get him noticed."

He didn't have an answer for that. The guy was a bum and his career tanked as soon as the news came out that Shelby was no longer seeing him. Mike saw the cell phone on the table in front of her. Face down. He pointed at it because talking about Shelby's ex-lover was starting a slow, angry sizzle somewhere near his heart. Time to get back to business. "Can I take a look?"

Her voice wavered a tiny bit. "It's really bad."

Mike had the absurd urge to scoop her up, blanket and all, and put her in his lap. She looked so sad and small, all bundled up and shut away from everything. One touch might shatter her hard-won composure, though, and he didn't want to do that to her. Instead, he grabbed the phone from the table. The video was loaded and ready for viewing.

And she was right. The images were worse than the original crime scene.

Shelby's hand had obviously started shaking during the recording, but the footage was steady enough to get the gist.

35

Another warehouse, but he couldn't determine the actual size from the small screen. The focal point was a bed. And the woman lying there.

She was naked, with a black satin sheet covering her breasts and genitals. The full-sized bed had splashes of red covering the edges of the mattress that had clearly dripped down to pool on the concrete floor. The illusion was a bed floating on a red pond.

The victim's eyes were gone. Removed cleanly displaying little blood or damage to the orbital sockets. Her lips were bright red, matching the color of the substance pooled beneath the bed.

And her throat had been cut all the way across. Mike could see the white bone of her spine. Curly blond hair completed the picture and then the music started. Shelby's third song off her first album. That album had gone platinum. And if he remembered correctly, the video had taken place on water, with Shelby rolling around on a bed singing about her lover being away.

"Can you tell where she is?" she asked.

Mike played it again, focusing on the background this time and not the body at the center of the shot. Finally, he shook his head. "Could be any of a hundred different places downtown. He could have even moved to one of the surrounding cities like Glendale or Peoria."

"That poor woman," she whispered.

"I'm forwarding what you have to one of my detectives. They'll go over the video frame by frame to determine a possible location."

"What about the first one? Do you know who she is yet?"

"We're waiting for the autopsy. We've got the prints done and dentals, but it's a matter of matching them up to missing persons. And if she was someone he grabbed from the street, then identification might take longer if she doesn't have a record."

"Why is someone doing this?"

"To get your attention. Something set this guy off. What's changed in your routine lately? Or in your life?" He saw her glance away and stare out the window. "This guy thinks he knows you, intimately. He's playing back your love songs and setting up his own sick little video homage to you. He's been watching you, Shelby. Fantasizing about *you*. He wants something from you that only he knows about. We can only guess. So the question is, why now? What happened to make him snap?"

Shelby pushed off the blanket and stood abruptly. She swayed but steadied herself. "I'm not sure, but I need to show you something. It might or might not be relevant. I have a secret of sorts."

"Is that even possible?" Mike asked.

Shelby smiled grimly, knowing he was trying to lighten the mood. "I've found that if you have enough money, almost anything is possible."

When she was sure her legs were steady, she moved toward the French doors that led back into the interior of the house. "House" was a silly word to describe the place. Showpiece was more apt. Filled with artwork and marble and elegant furniture, it lacked the warmth that made a home. The structure was someplace big enough to house her security team and Madge comfortably. As for Shelby, she could have done with a bit less extravagance.

"Come with me." She looked over her shoulder at the man sitting on the arm of the couch. He should have looked out of place in his jeans and rumpled t-shirt. The band named on the front of his shirt was *Rage Against the Machine*, which was ironic since Mike worked in one of the industries that particular band railed against lyrically.

But he didn't look out of place. He moved silently, his face set in hard planes. He towered over her, causing a delicious little shiver. He could have been a millionaire playboy for all the notice he gave of his surroundings. As if he'd been raised with that kind of wealth—but he hadn't been. He wasn't impressed, and he never would be. Mike didn't care about money. He cared about right and wrong.

"Tell me about this secret, Shel."

She shook her head. "It's better if I show you." So she led the way to the staircase and went up to the second floor. Mike was right behind her when she stopped in front of a door. The lights were off in this part of the house, so the hallway was dark, but when she opened the door the room glowed inside.

The glow came from all the stars hanging from the ceiling, as well as the nightlight. Shelby didn't look back at Mike, not sure what his expression would say. Instead, she walked toward the bed and the little figure sprawled out on top of the covers. Wearing the latest Pixar characters, the little girl had kinky-curly blond hair, pink lips that looked like cotton candy, and when her lids were open, sky blue eyes.

"This is my daughter."

CHAPTER 5

"Can you focus on that back corner?" Daniel asked.

When the call had come, Daniel hadn't been asleep, and he hadn't been alone. The woman in question was a friend with fantastic benefits. They met from time to time to scratch the itch—an arrangement that worked well for two career-driven workaholics not willing to devote time or energy to an actual relationship.

Now he was in the office with one of the lab techs who hadn't been asleep either. Lance Avery was one of those guys interested in all things techie. He played with the video Mike forwarded, enhancing as much as he could.

Daniel had already watched the video several times, each time searching for something new. Now he focused on everything about the space the girl was in, but the walls were bare. Nothing about the architecture stood out. The warehouse was likely just as generic as the first crime scene. "Damn, I was hoping for something useful."

Lance shrugged, still playing with his system. "Give me a couple minutes. I want to zoom in on the right side. Something over there is blurry."

Daniel saw the dark blur. About six feet high, it could have been a stack of barrels. Or crates. Smack in the middle of the blur was a white strip. Daniel moved closer to the screen. They had a still image from the video projected onto a wall in one of the bigger offices.

"Could be a label," Lance said, squinting up from his computer.

Damn, it could be. Daniel tried to quell the excitement. He still couldn't read it. "Any way to enhance the shot further?"

"Hey, this isn't *CSI*—that computer shit they do isn't even real. I can only focus so much before I lose everything and it becomes one big pixel nightmare."

Running a hand through his hair, Daniel nodded. "I know, man. But something's got to give. We have to find the crime scene before the fucking rats get there."

"Rats nothing. Have you *seen* what those feral cats can do?"

Daniel grinned. "Dog person, huh?"

"Hell yeah. If I die, I don't want my pet eating off my face, and those cats will. Dude, the moment you die, you're nothing but kibble to them."

The image cleared a bit more and it was a stack of crates. The thick white stripe was still blurry, but Daniel could make out a logo of some kind. "What is that?"

Avery had a magnifying glass over the screen of his computer. "Maybe a crown or hat of some kind? I can't make it any bigger, or we lose the image altogether." He held out the magnifier to Daniel as he scooted back to make more room.

Skirting the desk, Daniel moved closer to Avery's screen. With the image magnified, it did look like a crown, but with three lines to the right and some letters that were too close together to make sense of. "Can you screen shot this? I'll probably go blind looking at logos, but I know I've seen this somewhere."

Hearing Avery busy tapping on keys, Daniel wandered back to the larger image. *Who are you?*

But the victim couldn't tell them anything, except who she was . . . eventually. Maybe that would help, maybe it wouldn't. If she was indigent, then she was a random target that fit the killer's needs. But if she wasn't, then tracking her movements in the days before she was taken might provide useful leads.

"Oh shit."

Daniel turned at the exclamation, eyebrow raised, armed crossed. "What?"

Avery was almost vibrating with triumph. Still tapping away on his computer, he turned his monitor and pointed. "I know what that symbol is."

Tara Shumway was finally off shift.

He was waiting. He watched as she pulled the tie from her hair, letting the red corkscrew curls loose and running both hands through her head. He thought he could hear her moan at the release of all that hair.

Leaving the lobby of the emergency room, Tara glanced around before heading into the parking garage. The night had been busy, and that she was looking forward to getting out of her scrubs and into a bubble bath. He'd heard her conversation with a co-worker while they were on a break.

It was two a.m., and a good time to hunt. The voice was quiet, and he could focus and maintain the control he needed to use his disguise.

She held her purse close, keys in hand, like she did every night—keeping her head up and her body alert. Tara's daddy had taught her well, and she was always vigilant. He knew all about her, and she talked about her Daddy often. But his warnings wouldn't help her. Not tonight.

"Excuse me?" His voice startled her into a little jump.

She turned, wide blue eyes blinking into focus. She'd been deep in thought and not paying attention.

Daddy would be disappointed. *So careless.*

He stood a couple feet away with a smile and a confused look on his face. Women always thought he looked harmless. Like a lost puppy in need of looking after. The blue scrubs he'd worn, plus the sling on his right arm, completed his masquerade. At medium height with medium brown hair and medium brown eyes, he blended in. Average is what someone would say.

That was his biggest disguise, because when he looked in the mirror, he saw something else. Something darker than mere flesh. It scared him, but he was accepting it. And he could even forget about that reflection when he was working. Like he was now. "I'm sorry, I didn't mean to startle you."

Tara shook her head, eyeing his scrubs. "My fault, I was lost in thought. Do you work here?"

He nodded. "It's actually my very first shift, and I'm not sure where to go. You look like you know your way around, so I was hoping you could point me in the right direction?"

Smiling, Tara relaxed her shoulders and let her hand with the keys fall to her side.

He wasn't a threat in her mind.

"I got lost my first day, too. What department are you working in?"

"I'm assigned to the burn unit. For whatever good I am." He smiled, pointing to his injured arm. "Can you believe I slipped and fell right after I got hired?"

"That bites. But there's always a ton of filing to do, so I'm sure they'll still put you right to work." She wrinkled her nose. "I did a turn in that unit and was glad to get out. That smell really never leaves your clothes." Stopping, she grimaced. "But I shouldn't have said that."

He shook his head and moved closer. "Thanks for the warning. Getting advice is good. My name is Bobby, by the way," he said, holding out his left hand awkwardly.

"Tara," she replied, shuffling her keys to her other hand so she could shake his. "Nice to meet you. Is this your internship? You look a bit young to be an R.N. yet."

Her eyes widened and she took a step back. He couldn't help it, he was happy and his face must have changed. Grabbing her hand, he jerked her off balance and into his body, right over his sling. He slammed the hypodermic needle into her shoulder, and he could tell she hadn't made sense of what was happening yet. Her legs wobbled and when she tried to ask what he was doing, nothing came out. She stumbled backward against her car.

"Don't worry, Tara. I'll take good care of you. Just because I look young doesn't mean I don't have experience. I'm going to make you famous. Won't that be fun?"

Legs giving way, Tara's eyes crossed as she slid down, landing on her butt—hard. She finally realized what the sting was, he could tell. Plus he held the needle up so she could see it. She opened her mouth to scream, but nothing happened. No movement and no sound. Then her eyes slid closed.

Bobby easily lifted the woman and hefted her over his shoulder. He had his place set up with his favorite toys, just waiting for her. He hummed a song by Shelby Lynn and set off toward his Camry. The trunk was fitted for these little adventures. "I'm going to have so much fun with you, Shelby."

Tara made the tiniest sound before her body went limp, and she lost consciousness.

~

"SHE LOOKS JUST LIKE YOU," Mike whispered. And he wasn't sure how he felt about that. "That's one helluva secret to keep from so many of your adoring fans, for what five years?"

"Seven. Rebecca just had her seventh birthday last month." Shelby fussed over the little girl for a moment before ushering them both back out and into the hallway.

Mike wasn't sure what to say next, and he wondered how she could have done it. Hide a pregnancy and delivery. But he stayed quiet and followed Shelby into another bedroom. This one was hers. He could tell instantly. The room smelled like her and the clothes lying in haphazard piles all over the furniture were all classic Shelby. "I see fame hasn't changed you all that much either."

She shrugged, unselfconscious about the clutter. "One of the reasons I wanted to be rich and famous, remember? So I wouldn't have to clean up after myself." She smiled and opened the door that lead out onto the balcony. "I still suck at all the domestic goddess stuff."

"Not everyone is cut out for it."

The balcony was at the back of the house and gave a close-up view of Camelback Mountain. Not the view he would have guessed she'd pick. Especially since she'd seemed transfixed on the city lights while she was on the couch in the den.

"I feel safer here with the mountain at our back. An illusion, I realize, but it makes me feel better." She took a seat in a padded lounge chair and waved Mike to the one next to it. "And don't worry, the security team patrols the area here as well."

"She's not your daughter, is she?" Shelby didn't look surprised that he'd guessed.

"She looks like she could be mine. And now she is."

"Is she adopted?"

"Not yet, but after this tour is done, I'll file the paperwork."

"You didn't kidnap her, did you?" His tone was only half joking. She didn't have a mean bone in her body, and cold-blooded kidnapping was something she just wasn't capable of. At least the Shelby he used to know wouldn't have been able to. This Shelby was stronger, more capable than the young girl who'd left Arizona, and him, behind.

She looked up at him with a sad little smile and shook her head. "Oh, I'm her legal guardian. And her godmother as well. I was there the moment she took her first breath."

He sat down opposite her chair and leaned forward with his elbows on his knees. "Something tells me there's a story there. She's a cute kid." Then he settled in to wait. Mike was curious about how Shelby, with all her fame, could have actually hidden the child from the public.

"I've always said that I've led a charmed life. Nothing too bad has ever happened to me, not really. But some people have nothing but back luck and trouble. My friend Abby was one of those."

She splayed her hands out with a little shrug, as if questioning the Universe about how this could be.

And then with a shake of her head she continued. "I met Abby about a year after I got to Nashville. She and I shared a tiny studio apartment and waitressed during the day for money."

Her eyes took on a soft glow, and Shelby had ceased to be in the room with him. She was somewhere in the past, seeing her friend.

Shelby reached up and snagged one of her curls, pulling it down. Stretched out to full length it was long, reaching past her breasts. But when she let it go, it sprung back into place. A perfect corkscrew that only hung past her collarbone.

"We had the same hair, even though I was short and she was tall. It's what made us instant friends. We could talk for hours about the problems of trying to straighten it, and what the humidity did to it. You know—girl stuff."

"And Rebecca has the same hair."

Shelby focused on him again and the nostalgic smile faded. "Same color, same texture. Abby could have been my older sister, we were that close."

"How did you get a music contract?"

"Madge," she said. "Her dad was a career Army Ranger, and she'd been all over the world by the time she was a teenager. She became a talent agent in her thirties and made a name for herself by the time she turned forty. She heard me singing one day on a street corner."

"And signed you on the spot?"

Shelby chuckled. "Well, not on the spot. She took Abby and I under her wing, and a few weeks later, I was sitting with a professional voice coach singing scales, and Abby was enrolled in a cosmetology school, learning how to do hair and make-up. Madge says she just knew I would be someone special, and she knew I wasn't leaving Abby behind."

Mike was impressed. But then, Shelby had always been special. Whether she was on stage or sitting with no make-up in a padded lounge chair, she exuded charm. She'd been that way her entire life and, if he was honest with himself, he'd always known she needed to share that charisma with the world. He'd just thought he'd be with her when it happened. He gave himself a mental kick to stop the mopey thoughts. "What happened then?"

"I worked my ass off for a year before I got that first contract. My single came out, and six months later, my life was a rollercoaster ride."

"And what happened to Abby?"

Shelby played with another curl. "She came with me. As

my personal hair dresser and make-up artist. She was brilliant, and we were like kids playing dress up. All the gorgeous clothes and top-of-the-line cosmetics. The food was expensive and tasted better than anything either of us had ever experienced."

"But?"

"But Abby was lonely." Shelby let go of the curl and stood. She walked to the rail and leaned out.

For someone so famous, Mike thought Shelby was the lonely one. The way she held herself and the way she sank into the furniture, as if she were trying to disappear completely.

Shelby turned and crossed her arms. The night was still hot, but she rubbed goose bumps away as she stared back at him.

"I was always busy and didn't notice it when she started disappearing at concerts, or during the tour. She got secretive, and that just wasn't the girl I knew."

"She started seeing someone?"

Shelby nodded. "Abby wouldn't tell me who, but she seemed so happy, and I couldn't blame her. I just didn't have time for dating or anything besides my career and all the appearances and studio time. I barely had time to write my songs, and when I'd get off stage, I was dead to the world for the next twelve hours. I should have made more time for her. For us."

"So it was easy for Abby to have a secret affair without anyone knowing." Mike figured Abby enjoyed the secret, something to keep away from a friend that was having so much success. It was human nature to try and take something for herself.

"I think Madge knew there was a relationship, but even she didn't know who it was, and we both worried about it. And then Abby started smiling less. Her fun, short, summer dresses turned into a long drab skirts, and she started jumping every time the door opened or closed."

"Long sleeve shirts and heavy make-up as well?" He knew where this was going.

Again she nodded. "And stories about sudden clumsiness when she was one of the most graceful people I knew. I begged her to tell me who he was, because he had to be someone on the tour. But she wouldn't. And by that time, she was pregnant."

"Did he kill her?"

A tear slipped down her face as she flinched and took a small step back. "I honestly don't know. She had Rebecca, and the secret meetings stopped. No more bruises, and she seemed so happy. That lasted for six years. Rebecca made Abby complete, and they made everyone smile just to see them together." Shelby started to pace.

"Then one year ago, Abby left Rebecca with Madge, saying she had some errands to run. She never came back. I called the police, but they found no evidence of foul play. She simply disappeared, and they said it happens like that with some people. They just get up and leave their families and friends with no word. But they're wrong. If they'd ever seen Abby with Rebecca, they would've known she'd never willingly leave her daughter. There's just no way."

"What happened then?"

"I hired a private investigator to look into her disappearance." She hugged herself and turned back toward the mountain. "He couldn't find anything either. Like a black hole, one day she was here, and the next day, she just ceased to exist."

Mike could hear the frustration and hopelessness in her voice. "Did your manager run background checks on everyone connected to the tour?"

"Of course," she said, turning back to face him again. "And nothing came up. No huge red flag with a previous assault or a history of being an abusive asshole around any of my people. But at the time, we were touring with a couple of other bands and were headquartered in Nashville. We didn't have access to the names of everyone around, and then there was the possibility that the boyfriend was some local guy who followed the tour."

"You get that often? Folks following the tour?"

"Oh yes, and most of the time they're harmless. It's not that cliché female rock groupie that you see in the movies either. I have everything from older couples to bikers and college kids following my concerts from state to state."

"And no one stood out to either you or Madge?" Shelby's face was a mask of misery.

"I was too busy to notice."

Mike resisted the tug he felt. He refused to go and give her the comfort she so clearly needed. But denying himself was hard. Instead, he stayed in character and asked questions. From his seat. "Did you question Rebecca? Ask her if she'd seen anything or heard anything her mother said before she left?" A quiet sob escaped the woman standing so rigidly in front of him.

Another tear took the same path as the first one, and she crumbled.

Mike's resolve left him in an instant, and he couldn't keep away from her, from the heartbreak written all over her.

And then she was in his arms.

He swept her up and carried her back inside. Her whole body shook, but she stayed quiet, holding in the tears and trying not to touch him, even though her body was plastered against his. He carried her to her bed and sat with her still in his lap. Just like he'd wanted to do earlier. "I'm sorry about your friend, Shelby."

She took a deep shuddering breath. "I just wish I knew what happened. For myself and for Rebecca." She pulled away to look into his eyes, not even seeming to realize she was in his lap. "That little girl hasn't spoken a word since I had to sit her down and tell her that her mom was missing. In every way except blood, she's like my own daughter. She even used to call me Mama Two," she said, holding up two fingers. "Not until she was about three did I started having her call me Aunt Shelby. Abby deserved to be the only one being called Mom."

"And knowing for sure that she's dead will help you both?"

Shelby jerked out of his arms and almost jumped off his lap in a violent objection to his words.

Not that he'd said them harshly, but just saying the word out loud was enough. She'd used the words missing and disappeared, but she was hiding from the truth. Her friend was likely dead.

"What I feel doesn't matter. The only thing that matters is helping Rebecca. I helped raise her, and I love her almost as much as Abby *does*. I have to keep her safe, and we have to know what happened."

Does, not did. Stubborn to the end. But she had changed. She'd grown up while she'd been off getting rich and famous. That she valued someone other than herself was clear. Her feelings showed in the way she talked about her friend, the sincere regret that she didn't make time for her. And in the love shining through her eyes when she talked about Rebecca. Even Madge had a piece of her heart.

"Then I'll do everything in my power to make sure nothing happens to either of you," he said. And he meant it. Nothing and no one would hurt a little girl who was mute in her sorrow over her missing mother. "Just realize that you may never know what happened to Abby. And that's something you'll have to face sooner or later. For both your sakes."

"I'm sorry about all of this, Mike."

He shrugged. "I'd do it for any of my friends." Shelby looked like she wanted to say something but he got a text just then. He read it quickly and felt a leap of excitement. Daniel might have found the crime scene. Finally, something useful to do. "Listen, I have to go, but I'll be in touch. And if this bastard contacts you again, then call me immediately."

He waited until she nodded and then he left. It was a cowardly thing to do, running off to a crime scene when she'd opened up the way she had, but leaving was self-preservation. Shelby was the one chink in his carefully-built armored life. He couldn't afford to again get sucked into that particular whirlpool of emotion.

But he could solve this case. And then she could take off again. Because that's what she was good at.

CHAPTER 6

*A*s he approached the warehouse, Daniel cut his
lights. His police cruiser was one of the older Chevy
Caprices, so it was low to the ground and heavy. All the
police emblems had been removed so that it was considered
"undercover." But the searchlight mounted on the driver's
side door and more than one antenna on the roof made a
mockery of the term.

He circled the block slowly. The engine purred quietly,
making his approach as soundless as it could be. Nothing
moved in the pre-dawn hours. Even the homeless didn't
come down here at night. Between the rats and the isolation,
the location wasn't ideal if one wanted to stay safe. There
was no way the suspect was still there, but Daniel wasn't one
to rush into something.

Not after that rookie move had gotten him shot.

Thank God, he'd had his vest on at the time, but it hadn't
been one of his finer moments. And it had made him look
like a fool in front of the very beautiful woman he was trying
to save, not to mention her giant boyfriend. Now husband.

Pulling back around to the front of the building, he

parked so he could see the doors as well as the street. Mike was on his way now, and Daniel was glad. They didn't want patrol fucking up the crime scene if this was really the building. If it wasn't, then they didn't want to pull resources from the street on a hunch. It was a gut call, but he'd made it and Mike would back him up.

He sat for about twenty minutes before he saw headlights headed his way. He ducked down slightly, making himself less visible, in case the driver wasn't Mike. But the lights cut out about the place Daniel had cut his, and the big truck pulled up and stopped about twenty feet from his spot.

He grabbed his Mag light and keys and stepped out of his vehicle.

Mike did the same, unfolding his large frame from the seat, light in hand.

Daniel knew Mike's friends called him 'Little' Mike, but the guys on the department called him Tank. Not to his face, only when they talked about him. And he was. The man was made of muscle.

"What do we have?"

"A good gut feeling," Daniel answered.

Mike looked around and then back. "You've checked out the perimeter?"

"I have. Nothing moving anywhere in about a block radius, and I waited approximately twenty minutes before you got here. I never heard a thing, and it's so quiet here I'd have heard a rat fart."

"Then let's check out this theory of yours."

"Jesus, I hope this is it. We need to find this vic," Daniel said as he turned on his light. They neared the building on silent feet. Both used the light to sweep the ground in front of them, as well as the building.

"This is it," Mike said.

They hadn't made entry yet. "What makes you sure?"

"The smell."

His tone was grim, and Daniel had to wonder if the man had super senses as well. Because *he* didn't smell anything but dust and old diesel fumes. He inhaled as quietly as he could, but he still didn't smell anything out of the ordinary. So he shrugged and followed his boss to the door that, up close, was slightly ajar.

Mike pulled his gun out of his holster and Daniel followed suit, taking up a position behind his boss.

And then Mike opened the door.

The hinges should have made some kind of noise, as old as they were, but the door swung silently open. Mike was clearly thinking the same thing since he had his light shining on the jamb. He pointed.

Daniel could see a small dried pool of fluid, probably one of those spray lubricants, on the concrete stoop.

Without a word, they made entry.

And the smell hit Daniel. Just no mistaking the odor of a decomposing body. The metallic copper scent of blood hung heavily in the air as they swept the corner of the room. Daniel swallowed hard, attempting to ward off nausea. The room they were in was empty, but there was a door on Mike's side.

In the semi dark, Mike's serious face took on a sinister quality. Daniel was glad the big man was on his side, because he'd hate to go up against him. They were through the door into a maze of smaller rooms. Half-assed cubicles that were only partially dismantled. He could hear tiny rodent nails scraping across the floor, avoiding the light he swept through each area.

One more door in the back stood wide open and led into the large warehouse behind the offices. And there she was. Exactly as the video depicted.

"Good job, Daniel."

"I'm just glad this wasn't a colossal waste of time. We needed to find this scene."

"And now we need to call in the troops. I want this kept as quiet as possible."

Daniel nodded. "You think it was one of us? That news leak."

"Hell no," Mike said, walking slowly around the pool of shiny red liquid that coated the floor. "One of the rookies on patrol was probably thinking with his dick, and let slip the details of the scene to a reporter. Hope he got laid because if I find out who it was, he won't ever be able to use it again."

"I'll go and make the call," Daniel said. The job was his, but he couldn't deny getting away from the overwhelming stench of the room was his goal as well. The sight of blood was fine, but the smell was something else.

He turned at the door to ask if Mike wanted anyone in particular to respond, but he stopped when he got a look at his face. The high windows let in the moonlight and partially lit the room. Mike stood at the edge of the pool of blood, staring down at the woman on the bed. Pure rage was written on his face, as if the woman was known personally, and he'd been unable to prevent her death. There was pain as well. But where that emotion came from, Daniel couldn't fathom a guess.

Then Mike moved and his face was once again in shadow.

Turning from the sight, Daniel could feel the menace. All from his boss. He hurried from the room and pulled out his cell once he was free of the building. He dialed dispatch, thinking to himself that the man he'd just left wasn't a present-day homicide detective, but a throwback to another age where revenge and retribution was handled at a personal level.

Permanently.

Daniel would have to work harder to find this perpetrator, because if Mike found the killer first, there might not be anything left for the courts to prosecute.

~

THAT CASEY HENDERSON was more excited about getting called to a crime scene than she'd been about the date she'd had that night was a sad state of affairs. And the fact she was still strapped into a tight leather dress with five-inch heels, adding much-needed height, wouldn't stop her from heading straight to the scene. She carried a fairly large collection kit in her trunk, as well as an extra pair of her favored coveralls for work, just for these incidents.

There was nothing she could do about her favorite heels but try and not get blood on them. She'd have to remember to stash an extra pair of work boots in the trunk next time. And since this perp was the same sickie that set up the first scene, this one would more than likely be a doozy.

She parked her Charger on the street next to a big F-250, grabbed her camera from the case she carried and got out. She wanted to photograph the scene first before she had to suit up and take samples. And she hoped one of the on-duty guys for her office was already on the way, because she'd let her co-workers handle the heavy lifting.

Stepping carefully to avoid the cracked concrete, she picked her way through the overgrown weeds and glass that littered the sidewalk. She didn't want to nose dive into the parking lot because one of her heels got stuck in a crack.

"I'm sorry, lady, but you can't be here."

Casey looked up to see a plain-clothed detective standing in her way about midway to the warehouse. "Excuse me?"

"This is a police matter. And we won't allow the press inside. You should know that."

His tone rankled, like he was talking to an errant child

escaping from the romper room. Good thing she wasn't armed because she might have shot him, just for the tone. Clearly, he was new.

Giving him a scathing look, she weighed her options of getting around him without explaining who she was. But the heels were problematic. "Who says I'm press?"

He frowned at that.

She was glad. Casey reluctantly admitted the guy was cute. Tall, but with a thinner build than most of the cops she was used to dealing with. Not that he was skinny—no—he was well muscled. He had serious blue eyes that contrasted interestingly with sandy brown hair that would look great tussled after sex. She noticed he was giving her a thorough once-over as well.

While he liked what he saw, his gaze remained serious and he was still frowning. "I guess you could be a hooker with a hard-on for crime scenes."

She burst out laughing because it was such an outrageous thing to say. Casey didn't even take offense at being called a hooker, especially since her heels were fuck-me red to match her lipstick. He clearly hadn't seen the local flavor if he thought the Phoenix hookers took this much time with hair and make-up. Seeing a shadow over the new guy's shoulder, Casey peeked around to see Mike. "You gonna help me out over here? Your rookie thinks I'm a hooker."

"High-priced call-girl maybe, but hooker?" Mike's eyebrow was raised.

Casey smiled at him and shook her head. "At least it's more accurate. You call—I'm a girl—here I am. All dressed up and unable to get to the body because Deputy Do-Right here is blocking my way."

"Daniel Wolfe meet Casey Henderson, senior medical examiner." Mike made the introductions. "You look great, Case, sorry to pull you out of whatever you were doing."

"No worries, Mike. My date was a dud." She tossed her keys to the cute detective saying, "Be a doll and grab my case out of the trunk, will ya?" Then she swept around Detective Wolfe and followed Mike toward the building. By then, she was all business. "I expected more patrol cars. Who found the body?"

"Your errand boy. He played a hunch off a video feed our suspect sent to a witness. Turns out he was right. We've got a couple of patrol units enroute now to secure the perimeter, but they're not coming inside so the scene has stayed as pristine as I could make it."

"New guy has some chops, huh?"

Mike nodded. "He's a good guy. Came over a couple of weeks ago from burglary where he was making a name for himself. This is his first homicide investigation."

"He's cute."

"Well, I'm not really into guys, so I'll take your word for it. And if you start talking about his ass or package, I'm leaving you alone with the rats."

She laughed as she followed Mike though the remains of an office space and out into the warehouse. The smell was enough of a warning that she knew her heels were toast. When they stepped into the warehouse and she saw the poor girl lying on the bed without any eyes, Casey got mad. "I'd like to peel off this asshole's face while *he* squirms."

"Stand in line," Mike muttered.

"This is Shelby Lynn's third video, isn't it?" She'd made a point of looking them up after the first murder.

Mike nodded and moved to the side.

She would need more light, but she could take the initial photos relying on her flash. Casey paused, "This guy has a serious fetish for Shelby Lynn. I hope she has massive security."

"She does, but this is worse than just a fetish. He's sending her email videos of the crime scenes while they're fresh."

"Shit." She moved as close as she could to the bed without actually stepping into the red mess on the ground. "Is it just me, or does this feel like this wacko is going serial?"

"Three bodies by the same killer makes a serial killer, correct?" Daniel's voice cut into the gloom.

Casey turned and saw that he had her kit. "That is the accepted number," she replied. "But the cooling-off period is very quick for this guy. Two days between bodies is fast. Either he's done this before, or he's got a time frame in mind."

"But we don't know how long he's had the women yet," Mike chimed in. "So the time frame could be longer. Plus he waited until Shelby got to town to begin his little fantasy re-creations."

"Why the videos?" Daniel asked. "I mean, what's the point of re-creating them and sending them to her?"

"Being sick and twisted isn't enough?" Casey said it offhandedly as she circled the bed in the center of the room.

"Not usually. Even the crazies have a reason for what they do, even if we don't know what it is. What do you think, Mike?"

Casey stopped taking pictures and focused on Mike. He stood with his hands in his pockets looking around, taking in the scene. His posture was relaxed, but she'd worked with him enough to realize that under his laid-back attitude was a man who took homicide personally. The only thing that gave away the anger simmering underneath was the tick in his jaw that betrayed how his teeth were clenched. She'd found Mike to be smart and good at puzzles, especially when the case seemed hopeless. So she was curious about his take on the psychopath.

"This is about the message in the songs. Our boy wants to

believe Shelby Lynn is singing directly to him. Maybe even writes her songs about them as a couple. He's showing he's been watching her, listening to her, and this is his way of wooing her."

"Jesus," Casey said. His voice was devoid of emotion, but the ring of truth was there. It felt right. And one thing that Casey had learned over the years was to trust her gut.

Mike went on with a seemingly carless shrug, "I checked with police records in Nashville. They don't' have any cases like this and she was based there for the last fifteen years, in between tours."

"So this guy was waiting for her to come home, because she's originally from here, isn't she?" Daniel said.

Mike nodded. "Born and raised. Could be coincidence that he picked this time and place, but now that she's close enough to touch, he's going after her sooner or later."

"Because he thinks they belong together," Casey said. A shiver slithered over her, and the hair on the back of her neck stood up. It was creepy to think about someone watching her that way. Thinking of her that way. Poor Shelby Lynn.

Mike's cell phone rang, and he turned away to answer it.

Casey would have to wait until they could rig up some lights to get better pictures. Glancing at Daniel Wolfe, she noticed he was breathing through his mouth. The pang of sympathy surprised her, but she went with it. "Why don't you walk me outside, Detective?"

He turned to her and nodded, blowing out a quick breath and matching his strides to hers. Casey thought he was relieved to get away from the smell.

The stench of death was something she was used too and reminded her of the work she loved, so the smell never bothered her. She was about to say something to break the silence, when Mike did it for her.

"We have a problem."

"What now?" She would already be up for too long processing this scene. She wasn't anxious to add more troubles to her list.

"We've got a missing woman."

Daniel ran a hand through his hair as he frowned. "Why are we getting the call? Shouldn't that be missing persons?"

Mike's brow was deeply furrowed as he looked at them both. "The woman was taken from a hospital parking lot and, with the exception of hair color and being a little taller, she could be Shelby Lynn's twin."

$\mathcal{T}$he afternoon sun woke Shelby as it lasered through a crack in the curtains. Her body had finally taken over and shut off her mind, allowing some much-needed sleep. The black-out drapes were pulled closed so only the clock on the nightstand told her how long she'd been out. She stretched and yawned, feeling her jaw crack as she woke up and took inventory.

Overall, she felt better. Less terrified than last night, and more determined than ever to end her public life. This concert deal was bringing in enough money to set up her and Rebecca for the rest of their lives. Not that she wasn't already wealthy, but she needed this last hurrah, as a goodbye to her dream as well as putting a period on her portfolio. Financial security for the future was what she and Rebecca needed. And this tour was giving her that.

But in the wake of the murders, she'd had Madge cancel all her remaining public appearances. Shelby would do three shows, making them the best she'd ever done, and then fade away from the spotlight. Her dreams had come with a higher price than what she earned. And she was ready to begin again. With a new dream. A better one.

Something moved in the corner of her eye and her head whipped around in alarm. Clothes were piled up on a plush reclining chair, and in the center of that flashed a pair of eyes. Shelby reached out and flipped on the lamp by the bed. "What are you up to?" she asked, shoving curls out of her face.

But the eyes only blinked and then little shoulders shrugged up and down delicately.

Shelby smiled and held up the covers.

The pile of clothes exploded into every direction as a little body shot from the chair and jumped into the bed.

Wrapping her arms around the girl, Shelby asked, "Did you already eat?"

Rebecca nodded and snuggled into Shelby.

They leaned against the headboard together, and Shelby wished Rebecca would chatter away like she used to. She'd been like a little monkey, always moving and talking and getting distracted. Now she was too still, too mute and very unhappy. And Shelby didn't have the first clue how to help her.

The psychologist they hired said Rebecca would start talking again in her own time.

"Any ideas what we should do today?"

Another shrug.

"You want to go out and look around? We could go shopping and get something to eat?"

A negative shake of the head.

Shelby sighed. She didn't mind staying in the house, but she was getting cabin fever. The only thing that stopped it from being worse was because the house was so damn big. She needed to rehearse, but she didn't want to leave Rebecca long enough to do it. Besides, her band had been with her since almost the beginning, and they were the best. They would be rehearsing, but they didn't actually need her there with them. Her band made her sound great, and they would continue to do so, even if she didn't show up. "How about swimming?"

That suggestion got a slow nod. The property boasted an enormous zero gravity pool on the property they hadn't tried out yet. Guess it was time to work on her tan.

Madge poked her head into the room and when she saw Rebecca curled up with Shelby under the bed covers, she came all the way inside. "I've been looking for this one. I hope she didn't wake you."

Shelby hugged the girl closer while shaking her head. "Nope, I woke up all on my own. Rebecca never made a peep, did you?"

That got a frown from the little girl and a small smile from Madge. Shelby had been told not to tip-toe around the fact that Rebecca refused to speak, or couldn't speak, due to the trauma of missing her mother. To treat her normally, including joking around. "We were thinking of going swimming, Madge. How about you join us?"

But the older woman shook her head. "I have more calls to make and some business to handle, but you two go ahead. I'll have the chef put a basket of snacks and sandwiches together. Unless you want breakfast, Shelby?"

"No, just fresh fruit and maybe cheese and crackers would be good for me."

"Would you like something special, Rebecca?" Shelby asked, knowing she wouldn't get an answer. And she didn't.

The little girl shifted away and left the bed. She moved slowly and deliberately, like an old woman, not the child she should have been.

Shelby wished for something she could do to bring a bit of joy back into her life. She'd tried everything from toys to secret trips to visit the world-famous mouse in both Florida and California, but nothing worked.

Madge ruffled her hair as she left the room and then turned to Shelby. "I've hired several Phoenix police officers in an off-duty capacity to patrol the grounds. They'll start tonight."

"Do you really think that's necessary? Our guys have been great and have handled everything so well."

"They're a security team, they've never dealt with a serial killer. This isn't the regular overzealous fan. This is more serious than anything I've ever seen before and it will ease my mind to have them around. Besides, our guys need to sleep sometime, instead of splitting their shifts and leaving us one pair of eyes short."

Shelby couldn't deny that added patrols would make her feel better, and supporting local officers was a great way to help them, while they helped her. Plus, her security guys were tired. They all were on edge these days. "You're right, Madge. The guys need some serious rest, and we could use the help."

"I'll go see the chef now. You girls have fun at the pool and wear some sunscreen."

Shelby smiled softly as Madge left the room. The older woman never had any kids of her own or even been married. Said doing so would have cramped her style, but she'd taken on Shelby and Abby as if she'd been a mother her entire life. And Shelby loved her for everything she'd done for them both. To her, Madge would always be more than a mere manager.

Mike stopped by the office even though today was techni-
cally the first of his three days off. He'd finally turned over
the early morning crime scene to Wolfe and Casey, although
the way those two are sniping at each other when he left
might have been a bad idea. But he trusted they could remain
professional long enough to gather all the evidence before
moving the body to the medical examiner's office.

He gave the day shift Sergeant the rundown of what he
had and left messages with dispatch to call him if they got
anything good. And then he left. A tip or actual eyewitness
would be a blessing, but Mike wasn't holding his breath. This
killer was good. Mike would have to be better.

In the meantime, it was time to make Shelby and Rebecca
disappear. When he arrived at the mansion on Camelback,
he and his truck were recognized and he was waved through
the gate.

Madge met him at the door. "You have news?"

He shook his head. "Not about the homicides, but a devel-
opment has occurred in the case."

"By the look on your face, I don't imagine it's good."

"It's not."

She waved him toward the large room that was serving as
a sitting area and office space.

The same place Shelby had been the night before when
she'd been staring off into the cityscape. He moved to the
window and noticed he could see the pool from where he
stood. More interestingly, he could see the people in the
pool.

Rebecca splashed around, but she wasn't smiling. That
poor little girl was lost and needed to find her smile again.
Madge said they were doing everything they could think of
to help her through it. He could see Shelby's head in the
water, as she watched the young girl. She smiled and laughed

and her mop of hair resisted the water's efforts to tamp it down.

"Alright, we are alone in here. Tell me what's going on."

"You did great by hiring some off-duty guys. I saw two at the gate and another one roaming the property outside. I'm guessing that was a suggestion from the Chief?"

Madge nodded. "It's was a good one, too. Our security team was tired and needed the rest. They'll take over again at night." She cocked her head at Mike and crossed her arms. "Tell me what's bad enough to come over personally."

Mike turned from the window and faced the woman standing by the couch. She was in tight jeans and a Tennessee Titan's jersey, which just made her seem broader through the shoulders than she really was. "There's been a kidnapping."

"And you think it's related?"

Mike pulled a picture out of his back pocket—a copy made by the missing person's detective assigned to the case. The smiling picture of a woman with corkscrew-curly strawberry blond hair and blue eyes a shade lighter than Shelby's own. Only a year or two younger as well. He handed it over. "This is why I'm concerned."

Madge hesitated and then took it from his hand. "Jesus Christ," she said. Then she sat on the couch arm. "When was this woman taken?"

"About the same time we were discovering the second crime scene."

Madge looked up from the picture and frowned. "So you actually found another scene? Was it just like the video?"

"Exactly the same. This guy is really getting a taste for it."

"Jesus," she muttered again.

"He's working his way up to Shelby herself. You understand that, right?"

"That poor girl." Madge stroked a thumb over the picture.

Then she raised a sad gaze to meet his. "What else can we do to protect Shelby and Rebecca?"

"I have a plan, but I need you on board before I approach Shelby because she'll look for your opinion, and I need it to match mine." Mike knew he looked hard and inflexible, but the woman in front of him gave him the same look. Nothing would happen unless she okayed it. And Mike respected her for it.

"Let's hear this plan."

He told her. And explained the where, the what, and the who, before providing a couple of phone numbers.

She gave him a narrowed-eye look. "Can you keep her safe?"

"I can. If, for even one moment, I felt she'd be safer somewhere else, that's where I'd take her. And if our boy is skilled enough to follow me, then he'll be in my playground, and that's a place he'll regret for the rest of his short life."

"I don't want a world of hurt—" she said quietly, "—I want dead. For Shelby and for those poor girls he mutilated."

"Yes, Ma'am. Understood."

SHELBY WAS WATERLOGGED. Even though Rebecca didn't smile, she splashed around and did handstands—everything that a normal happy child did while swimming. They'd taken a break and eaten some gourmet sandwiches with apple slices and caramel.

Rebecca was finally slowing down thirty minutes later when Madge called her name from the house. She climbed out and headed inside.

Shelby took the opportunity to do a couple of laps to work out the kinks. Taking off, she swam laps until her arms burned and her lungs begged for more air. Popping up, she whipped her hair out of her eyes and that's when she saw him.

Standing in the sun like some pagan warrior in jeans. He stood at the edge of the pool with his arms crossed, waiting patiently for her attention. She offered up a tentative smile. "I didn't know you were coming over today."

"It's not a social visit." He held out his hand.

She hesitated for a brief moment. Touching Mike was hard. Shelby felt things at a mere touch that she thought she'd never feel again. That reaction was dangerous to her peace of mind, not to mention her sudden clamoring libido.

But he stood patiently, hand out, waiting.

"I'll get you all wet," she warned.

"It's over a hundred degrees out, Shel. I'll dry without a problem."

So she reached up and his big warm palm enclosed hers and he pulled her, one-handed, from the water as if she weighed nothing. He wrapped a towel around her bikini-clad body faster than she could process the fact she was already out of the water.

She moved to the shade and sat on one of the chairs to dry out a little. "Have there been any new developments in the case?"

Mike sat across from her. He leaned over with his elbows on his knees and looked at her. "Something happened that needs immediate action."

His expression was one she couldn't really decipher. Her breath caught. "Another murder?"

"Not yet."

Shelby searched his face. She did and didn't want to know what he might say, but she couldn't help but ask. "What happened, Mike?"

"There's been a kidnapping. Unless we find that girl soon, she will be the third victim. We've got all the best detectives on the situation, plus a host of patrol officers that are solely dedicated to her case."

She gasped and put a hand to her mouth to somehow hold in the horror she felt. "How can you be so sure? I mean, are you positive it's related to what's happening now?"

After pulling the picture out of his pocket, Mike extended it.

She took it from his hand and quickly looked down. And immediately wished she hadn't. "Oh no."

"The resemblance is uncanny."

"He took her because she looks like me," she said it flatly. It was the only reason that made sense. "So what does this mean for us? I mean, Madge hired off-duty officers, so we have extra security. What else can we do?"

"Cancel the concert."

Shelby shook her head. "I can't do that. Not only would it be devastating to my fans, but that kills my plans for Rebecca. I need the money those concerts will bring."

He narrowed his eyes and frowned. "Is your life worth a pile of cash?"

"My life is about that little girl inside and anything I can do to make her life better, I will do. And that includes making sure these concerts go off perfectly so I can retire and take care of her."

He nodded, but the frown remained.

Shelby had an idea he'd already known her answer.

"Then I have an alternative for your safety and Rebecca's."

Shelby couldn't help but be wary. She was already in what she considered protective custody, what more could he want? Posting officers inside the house was out of the question, doing so would scare Rebecca. "What's your idea?"

"You and Rebecca come with me. Today. Now, as a matter of fact. I have a place up north that's secure. Only one person at the department knows where it is, and I can see anything that's coming. I can keep an eye on you and Rebecca, and you'll be safe until the concert."

Shelby shook her head. "I can't just run off with you to God-knows-where. I have to rehearse and prepare for the shows. The band needs me at some point, and a thousand different things still need to be done."

"And Madge will handle them all. This is non-negotiable, Shelby. I've already spoken to the Chief and the Mayor. Both agree getting you out of town would be best for the safety of the public."

"I'm considered a public menace?" That made her feel lower than a snake's belly—the thought that she was somehow bringing all this horror to the city she loved.

"It's a fact someone out there is obsessed with you to the point of killing innocent women to get your attention. While that isn't your fault, being locked up in a gilded cage that is easily accessible to this guy isn't wise. Especially since his cooling-off period is getting shorter."

Shelby swept around her hand, encompassing the house. "We have men with guns patrolling the grounds. How is that easily accessible?"

"This guy is clearly smart, Shel. He's methodical, meticulous, and patient. That is a deadly combination. Add that you're his ultimate target, and those are odds I don't like. I can protect you, but I want you and Rebecca on my home turf."

"How can you protect us better than my guys?"

"They don't have my training. I looked over their background checks. None have any military service, and none of them have ever been in a situation where they've had to take a life. That means they'll hesitate. And if they do, even if it's only a second, then people die."

"And you won't hesitate?" Shelby wanted to understand, because she was chilled by the hard resolve in his voice. He was serious, and he was deadly. She could see all of that written on his face and in his body language.

"No."

His intention was there, stark in its simplicity. He was telling her that he'd kill for her. Or maybe not her, maybe for the dead women or the woman that he was sure would be next. And even while the topic chilled her, his hard resolve warmed her heart. Truth was, she trusted him. Even after all these years, she knew deep down he'd always be that rock for her. And here he was proving it, yet again. "What about when I come back for the concert?"

"Extra security is already planned for the concerts. Checkpoints will be stationed at the entrance of the arena to make sure everyone coming and going gets a thorough search. A lot of that is normal procedure, but we'll have undercover officers there as well, milling in the crowd and looking for potential threats."

"I don't want anyone else hurt because of me."

"Then come away with me. Let me protect you both and get you out of reach. We need time for forensics to come back, and we need this guy to think you're still here, hiding out until the concerts. Security will remain in place and act normally."

"And you think that will work?"

"He's watching this place. Waiting for glimpses of you. We know that, otherwise he couldn't have followed your hairdresser to plant that letter. He'll think you're still here if everyone acts as if you are."

Shelby took a deep breath. She wanted to go with him, and not only because she was scared of this killer. She wanted to be with him, even if he was just acting as a bodyguard. The chance to be close to him was a temptation she didn't want to resist. She'd loved Mike once, but she'd walked away. As the years passed, she realized she'd walked away from the best thing she'd ever had.

Maybe this was her second chance. Or maybe it was the worst decision she could make, but she was doing it. Mike would protect her and Rebecca and make sure nothing happened to them. And if something...more...happened between them during the time away?

Well, a girl could always hope.

CHAPTER 8

"*N*ow listen," Zach Steele said above the noise. He was amazed that animals still came around their cabin in Flagstaff, with as much ruckus as the three kids made. And with his friend Mike's eminent arrival with Shelby Lynn, he needed to lay some ground rules. "I expect you kids to be nice. None of your usual shenanigans around this girl, Rebecca. Am I clear?"

Three heads nodded. The oldest boy grinned and gave a thumbs-up, and the twin girls just giggled.

"Did he just say shenanigans?" Jesse asked.

Zach heard him and glared at his best friend. "Now get outside and play." He dismissed the kids and turned to the three adults grinning from the kitchen table. "What?"

His wife, Elizabeth, smiled openly and gave him a wink. Her pale blond hair was piled lazily on her head, giving him an intriguing view of her very sensitive ear lobes. Zach might have to nibble on those later.

The view made him want to kick out everyone and kiss her. And maybe more.

"Just marveling over the new vocab word," Jesse said, his

grin stretching across his face. "I wasn't even sure you knew words over two syllables."

"You leave him alone," Lily said, punching the big man in the shoulder. Jesse's wife was unsuccessfully hiding her own grin. "Or I'll pull out the video of you changing the twin's diapers again. Zach loves that video."

"I think I'd like that," Zach said. "The sounds of Jesse gagging, along with the faces he made, would brighten my day."

"Hey, when did I become the bad guy?"

Lily laughed out loud and the gaiety made his Beth laugh as well.

Zach was possessive as hell, and didn't like sharing his family. But Beth and Lily with their pretty heads together laughing was just about the most beautiful thing he'd ever seen. He even put up with his best friend making fun of him.

"So what kind of trouble are we expecting?" Jesse asked.

"And who is the woman Mike is bringing home?" Beth asked. "He never brings anyone to his cabin."

"And we've looked," Lily said. Her grin was full of fun.

Zach sighed. He'd been putting off this discussion for as long as he could, but since Mike was arriving with his cargo in a couple of hours, he couldn't anymore. And the whole thing was going to be a pain in the ass. He really hoped this sick fuck followed them up, because then he'd have something interesting to do. And between him, Jesse, and Mike, there was no way in hell that asshole was leaving their mountain alive. End of story. End of problem.

He addressed Jesse first because he knew he'd never get a word in after he told the ladies who, exactly, was coming. "Mike's not really expecting any trouble. But just to be safe, we should make sure all the cameras are operational and put up a couple of perimeter trip wires for a bit of extra warning."

"Great," Beth said. "That means you'll stick Xavier and me

in the bunker if you see a scorpion, while you run around and play hero."

Jesse snorted, and Lily smiled. Then Jesse said, "How about Lily, the twins and I, go into the bunker with Xavier, and I give you my gun to help Zach?"

"Over my dead body," Zach growled. His heart did a flip at even the thought of his Beth being near another psycho. The first time it happened was enough to give him premature gray hair. Hence the bunker. But she was right, if he saw so much as a cross-eyed bear she and their son were going in. Nothing and no one was going near his family until he made sure it was safe.

"Tell us about the woman," Lily said. "What's she like? Has Mike talked much about her?"

Zach sighed. This was it. Time for the explosion. "He's bringing up Shelby Lynn with her adopted daughter."

Beth and Lily gaped in a moment of stunned silence. He really wished his wife would close her mouth, it was giving him ideas. He grinned.

Jesse stood and moved away, as if he too expected something.

And then it happened. Lily let out a shriek, and Beth finally closed her mouth.

"Shelby Lynn? The country singer?"

"How does Mike know her? Oh my god, this is so exciting."

"I won't even know what to say, she's so famous. And what's going on that Mike is expecting trouble?"

"I have to get out my Shelby Lynn CD collection so she can sign them."

"The twins will go insane with they see her, she's their favorite singer in the whole world."

The women were talking so fast to each other he wasn't even sure who was asking the questions. Zach looked at his best friend and nodded toward the back patio door. "Time to retreat, Marine," he said out of the side of his mouth.

Jesse nodded, and they both backed away from the happy whirlwind.

"Think they'll notice?"

"Nope."

They stepped outside to the sounds of a game of hide and seek coming from the side of the house. Zach poked his head around and found all three kids easily. They knew better than to leave the yard.

"So tell me the rest," Jesse said.

Zach filled him in on everything Mike had told him. He finished talking, and Jesse had a considering look on his face.

"Damon and Dani are home in Louisiana for a couple of weeks before she gets deployed again. Damon could easily run up to Nashville and take a look around."

Zach leaned back against the rail of the back porch. "I was thinking the same thing. From what Mike said, he doesn't think these murders and Shelby's friend going missing are related, but I'd like to know for sure."

"So would I. And Damon can get answers out of anyone."

"I haven't told the wives yet, but they're coming out for the concert."

Jesse smiled. "That's great. I want to give him shit about the dopey grin he always has in their pictures."

"We've all come a long way from where we used to be," Zach said.

"You mean pathetic men who couldn't dress themselves?"

"At least we don't have to go shopping anymore." Zach couldn't be happier, and he knew Jesse was just as content with his life. They were better men because of their wives and children, and Zach wouldn't trade his family for anything.

He knew about Mike and Shelby's past together. And he

wondered if maybe this was Mike's second chance at love. Zach, Jesse, and Damon had found the right woman at the wrong time, but then they all got a second chance. And so far, they were three for three in the love-conquers-all arena. He hoped he could add 'Little' Mike to that equation.

Mike deserved some happiness.

"YOU CAN BOTH SIT UP NOW."

Mike's voice from the front seat floated down to Shelby who was flat on her back with Rebecca lying in her arms. Mike had the foresight to pad the seat with a few blankets and a couple of pillows, so she was quite comfortable in her hiding spot. He had allowed them a single bag of clothes each, which he stowed on the floorboard of the back seat. He didn't want to chance them being seen in the bed of the truck.

Rebecca sat up, still sleepy from the swim.

Shelby climbed into the front seat and let her little girl lay back down.

She'd been playing a game on her tablet but for the last thirty minutes her eyes had started to droop. Before long she'd be out cold.

"You're sure we weren't followed?" Shelby asked.

"Positive." Mike's thumb tapped the steering wheel in time with the song playing on the radio as he drove.

"I thought you didn't listen to country music." She was surprised he put it on that station while negotiating traffic to get them out of town.

"I developed a taste for it some years back." He stared at the road.

But Shelby thought she heard a bit of humor in his voice. She bit back a smile. "I'm shocked. You actually like that twangy crap now?" Recalling his words to her years before got a tug of his lips, but not an actual grin.

"I've mellowed with age. Plus, seems country is the preferred music of the armed forces, so I was inundated with it during my tours."

"How many did you do?"

He glanced at her. "Two in the field, one at a desk."

"You don't seem like a desk kind of guy. I'm surprised."

"Not my choice, but I received an injury that prevented another active tour of duty."

"What kind of injury?" Shelby thought he looked as perfect as she'd ever seen a man. He didn't move with difficulty, but maybe the injury was something that couldn't be seen. She hoped it wasn't something that still caused him pain.

"I took a shot in the leg, but the problem was the bomb that went off at the same time. The shrapnel messed me up pretty good."

Shelby sucked in a breath and started to reach for him, but stopped short. "Dear God. Are you okay now?"

"I was okay then, just took too much time healing. They knew I had a knack for figuring out stuff, so I ended up in Intelligence as my punishment."

"I don't imagine that just anyone ends up in Intelligence, punishment or otherwise."

Mike shrugged and his hands tightened on the wheel.

He didn't like talking about it, but he was. Shelby hoped it was a good sign that he was willing to share his past with her. But she wanted to know so much more. "How do you like being a homicide detective?" Then she winced. "I mean, the job can't be fun, but with your knack you must've been a natural for the position."

He glanced at her and then back over his shoulder toward Rebecca.

Looking back herself, she could see that Rebecca was out cold. Her lips were parted and the tablet was still going in her little hands. She'd fallen asleep mid-game. Shelby unbuckled her seatbelt and reached back to turn it off. "You were saying?" she prompted as she settled into her seat.

Mike finally grinned at that point. "So nosy. But yes, I do enjoy my job. I like being the one to catch these people and put them behind bars where they belong."

"And do you have a woman in your life? Currently, I mean." Shelby hoped he didn't, not that it was a fair thought. She didn't have anyone, and so much time had passed since she'd had sex that she was afraid she was a born-again virgin. Worse, she was half afraid her libido had died.

That all ceased to be an issue when Mike walked into that conference room four days ago. Her body had revved to life in an instant, like she'd come out of hibernation. And she hadn't stopped thinking about the kiss. His goodbye kiss. It was fire and ice. A rather lethal combination.

Mike had yet to really unthaw with her, but it didn't stop her body from turning to an inferno every time he was near. "Normally, I'd say that I didn't mean to pry—but I do. I want to know about your life."

"I haven't been a monk, but no, there's no one current. What about you? *Have* you hidden a relationship from the press?"

Shelby shook her head. She didn't have time for one, much less want one. "I'm single, much to the distress of the paparazzi."

"Another reason I wanted you to hide out as we left your place. The last thing we need is this guy knowing where you are from some damn photographer out to get an exclusive."

"They are the bane of my life."

"I will keep you safe, Shelby. Nothing is going to happen to either of you while I am around."

But how long will you be around? "I know you will. I imagine you are trained in ways that I'll never understand, and you take it seriously. I couldn't feel safer."

"I appreciate the cooperation. I didn't want to use my trump card."

"And what was that?"

He gave her a quick glance. "You won't like it."

"I haven't liked anything about this situation, so you might as well tell me."

"We could have forced the Mayor to cancel your concerts, due to the risk to the public."

Shelby sucked in a little breath. That would ruin everything. "Well, I hope this little hiatus will help your people catch this guy."

"It might not, Shelby, so don't get up your hopes."

"I can't let you cancel those shows. I will fight you on it."

"Use your head for once. The money is not worth the danger involved. And what if someone gets killed there? We already have two dead girls and one that's missing."

"I have a duty to the fans—"

"Bullshit," he cut her off. "You have a duty to that little girl in the backseat. She's lost one mother already. She doesn't need to lose two."

Shelby didn't have a comeback for that statement, and they both knew it. Performing was a risk, but one she was willing to make for the life she had mapped out for herself and Rebecca. Besides, she would be perfectly safe. There would be tons of security, plus Phoenix police officers for crowd control.

She faced the window and watched the scenery. Mike wasn't overly talkative, so another hour passed before anything other than music interrupted the silence. Not that atmosphere was uncomfortable exactly, but it wasn't the kind of quiet that felt natural.

As comfortable as his truck was, Shelby couldn't wait to be outside stretching her legs. The higher in elevation they got, the cooler the air was outside. She could feel it on the window. The saguaro cacti and scrubby little acacia trees melted away as they drove, replaced by tall pine trees, slender birches, and the occasional oak tree. Not anything like the immense oak trees in Nashville, but a hardier version that could live with little precipitation. "I'd forgotten how much I missed Arizona."

"Scorching heat, no rain, Snow Birds every winter, and the never-ending shades of brown—what's not to love?"

Shelby smiled. "Mild winters, no snow to shovel, the Grand Canyon—I missed it."

"Arizona does have its finer points."

"You came back," she said. "You could have gone anywhere after the Marines, but you came back here. Why?"

He shrugged. "It's home."

Shelby felt the same way, but she took a bit longer to realize the restlessness that wouldn't go away was really a longing for home. A place that she missed, even while surrounded by the opulence of her lifestyle and the high energy of Nashville.

"You'll be meeting some friends of mine. They'll be extra eyes to make sure you and Rebecca are safe. Their wives and kids are excited to meet you."

She turned slightly to look at him. "Are you sure we should expose them to this danger?"

Mike threw back his head and laughed.

It was a wonderful sight and tugged at the corners of her mouth. She couldn't stop the silly smile.

"Just wait until you meet them, you'll see. It's going to be fine and Rebecca will have some kids to play with."

"They won't be mean to her because she doesn't talk, will they?"

Mike grinned, looking relaxed as he drove on. "Don't worry, it's better that she doesn't. The twins wouldn't let her get a word in edgewise, and Xavier will just drag her along with whatever he has planned. That kid is a natural leader, like his father."

"Well, then, I can't wait to meet your friends." Shelby couldn't help the nervousness she felt. She, who could sing in front of thousands of screaming fans, was nervous to meet Mike's friends. Mike was never the kind of guy to have a lot of friends. He much preferred being a lone wolf. That he could laugh and talk about these people with such affection was a wonder. They must be great people, and she didn't meet too many of those in her business.

She just hoped she lived up to their expectations. Most people only wanted to meet the superstar, never realizing she was just a "person" too. With her own insecurities, hopes, and dreams. Being an internationally acclaimed country singer was only one of those dreams, and recently the role had become more of a burden.

They turned off the main road and onto a dirt track where the trees were thicker. The sun was sinking into the horizon, and Shelby heard yawning from the backseat. She looked back and saw Rebecca was awake and sitting up.

She looked around and rubbed her eyes.

"We're almost there, honey," Shelby said. And sitting there, next to Mike and with Rebecca in the backseat, was like they were a regular family. Maybe getting away from the bustle of the city at their weekend cabin. It was nice.

It was normal.

But nothing about her life was normal. So maybe she could just pretend for a couple of days.

CHAPTER 9

here is she?
There was some extra security around her rental, but that big manager of hers had picked a bad spot. Oh, the house was nice enough if you were into big monstrosities of luxury. What interested him, though, was the mountain at its back. The other side of which was accessible to the public as a hiking trail. It was easy enough to walk along and then disappear around the other side.

From his vantage point, he could see the back of the house and into the room Shelby claimed. She liked the balcony, and he enjoyed watching her. When the time was right, it wouldn't be hard to take her from there.

He was getting anxious.

He wanted to reveal himself to the woman of his fantasies.

Time for her later. You have other things to do first, the voice said.

It was so loud in his mind that he actually turned, expecting to see someone there. But, of course, there was no one. So he ignored it. Not that doing so ever helped. The voice didn't like to be ignored. Re-focusing on the house, he wondered again where she was. He hadn't even seen the little girl. The god-daughter. The one that looked so much like her mother.

You pathetic little monster. Leave this, and get back to the woman you have. She's probably waking up by now.

"I know, but I wanted to see her."

Stop being weak. You have work to do. And she's almost perfect.

"She's not Shelby," he said, making her name a caress. "She's not the one."

One bitch is as good as another, the voice hissed. *They're only good for two things.*

"That's not true," he whined. He smacked his head, willing the voice to stop. Because he knew what was coming. The mantra. He'd avoided it for so long, but in the end, the voice was always right. He was weak. But not anymore. Now he was strong and in charge.

Say it, maggot. Say what the bitches are good for.

"No," he said. Then the pain started. He almost yelped as a sharp pinch started behind his eyes. "I don't want to say it. Just because you make me do things . . ."

I'm stronger than you are, and we both need it. The rush—the power—the satisfaction. So say it.

The pain increased until he was panting and sweating. He held out as long as he could, but in the end, he gave in. Like he always did. "Bitches are only good for fucking and killing."

And the new bitch is waiting.

"But I want to know where Shelby is."

You can come back after.

After, he thought. When the voice was quiet again. When he could control himself. Then he could watch Shelby for as long as he wanted without the voice being there. Without the pain and the cravings.

Without the shadow man.

85

~

"WOLFE," Daniel said as he answered the phone.

"Hey, it's Casey. We have the autopsy done for the second vic. You want to come down and talk it out, or you just want me to email you the report?"

"Just send it over."

"We found something interesting," she said.

Daniel was going blind reading the last autopsy report and wasn't thrilled about the new one, but it was part of the job and Casey had made it a priority due to the missing woman. But the lilt in her voice sounded interesting, so he leaned back and smiled. He liked the sassy little medical examiner.

"Yeah?"

"Yeah. And if you ask me nicely, I'll tell you what I found instead of just calling Mike directly."

"Your choice." Daniel made sure to sound as bored as he felt. He didn't play games and while he liked to imagine the smile on her face, he still wasn't that guy. The information was in the report and he'd find it. As soon as she sent it to him.

"You always have a stick up your ass?"

"You always insult the cops you work with?" He'd heard about her reputation. Casey Henderson was a ball-buster and her focus was cops. Maybe she'd dated one and it went bad, or maybe she just didn't like the general species. Whatever it was, about the only person she tolerated was Mike.

"Not always. But you certainly make it fun."

"Just sent the damn report."

She chuckled, "I was going to tell you anyway. I found a hair."

Daniel sat forward and put his elbows on his desk. "Tell me it was human and male?"

"Male," she confirmed. "But not human."

"Damn. Probably a dog, right?" And they had no way to track it. Not unless the animal was some crazy rare breed that was purebred and had papers. Then they—might—get lucky and be able to trace it.

"Not a dog. I wouldn't have bothered to call if it was a lousy dog hair."

"I'm all ears."

"So are these little guys. The hair comes from a chinchilla."

Daniel sat upright in his chair. "What the fuck is a chinchilla?" Her laughter at his total confusion didn't bother him as much as it should have. But he still didn't know what one was. He started pulling up a search engine on his computer and waited for her answer.

"It's basically a chubby South American ground squirrel. They're raised for their fur because it's reportedly extremely soft."

"So this critter is something rare?"

"Not rare exactly, but not a common pet for sure. I don't imagine there are that many stores that specialize in chinchillas or their habitat."

Daniel grinned, feeling a small ray of hope. This was something he could actually work on. The bastard had made a mistake, and that's all he needed to go with. "Thanks, Casey. This is great news."

"I thought you might like it. I just emailed you the file."

Then the line went dead, but Daniel didn't care. He started searching for pet stores that specialized in exotic rodents. Then he started making lists.

Finally, something to do other than stare at the same report.

~

THE CABIN WAS an A-frame in the front that stretched out into a ranch-style home. Its exterior was rough, with plenty of real wood logs completing the A. There was a barn in the back that went against the traditional red and white. Instead, the walls were green camouflage as if daring someone to say something.

It was a beautiful area and a lovely house.

Rebecca was up and looking around as the truck rolled to a stop.

The front door opened, and two of the biggest men Shelby had ever seen came strolling out. She glanced at Mike, but he was still completely relaxed. "Are they staying with us?" she asked. Neither had a smile on his face, and the dark-haired man was downright scary. The blond man was actually larger than the other, and they were both quite handsome. But something about the serious face on the brunette worried her. Possible bodyguards, but Shelby hoped not.

"No, but they live close by." Then Mike exited the truck and came around to open her door.

"The mean one scares me," she whispered low enough that Rebecca wouldn't hear.

Mike's eyebrow shot up, and he glanced over at the two men who had moved out into the yard but stood there like sentries, arms crossed and waiting. "The one with the dark hair?" he whispered back.

"I'm worried he'll scare Rebecca."

Mike just shook his head and held out his hand.

Shelby trusted Mike, but she was feeling very unsure at this moment.

He helped her out of the truck then he opened the back door and let out Rebecca. Taking her hand, he led them both over toward the cabin.

Jesus, Shelby thought, *these guys were even bigger up close.*

And that was saying a lot, because Mike was huge. He wasn't as tall, but he had muscles to spare.

"Shelby, these are my friends and Marine brothers, Zach Steele and Jesse Calhoun."

She contemplated if she should shake hands when there was suddenly some screaming.

Two of the most adorable twin girls ran out of the cabin and squeezed between the two men.

"You're Shelby Lynn," one of them said. They were dressed in jeans and matching blue shirts that made their blue eyes even bluer.

The only difference Shelby could see was that their blond hair was braided on different sides of their heads.

"Hi," the other one said. "You're our favorite." And then she hid behind the one Mike said was Jesse.

Then a mini-version of the scary one named Zach come bounding out of the house.

His chest was puffed out, and he was scowling like his father. "Dad," he called, "Mom says stop frowning, you're probably scaring the lady."

And the big man put his hands on his hips and stared down at his son. "Go tell your mother to come out here and tell me herself." Then he rolled his eyes and shook his head at Mike as his son ran back inside. "Women."

"The wives are inside stocking the fridge and the pantry," Zach said. "We weren't sure what you'd like so they bought out the damn store."

"Plus, they got a ton of girly stuff for you and little Rebecca here," Jesse said. He squatted down, and both of his girls crammed themselves up against his sides.

Shelby noticed Rebecca had done the same thing to her. The three girls were all looking at each other with big eyes and shy smiles, at least from the twins.

89

Jesse smiled and nodded at his girls. "Do you like horses?" he asked Rebecca.

Rebecca nodded, her little face solemn.

"This is Jennifer and Jessica, and they want to show you their favorite pony. Don't you girls?"

The twins giggled, and each held out a hand toward Rebecca.

The little girl looked up and when she saw Shelby nod, she reached out a hand slowly toward the grinning twins.

And that was all the invitation they needed. They grabbed Rebecca and started talking a mile a minute, starting and completing each other's sentences in that universal twin way that had Rebecca's head turning constantly to the one speaking.

"Are you sure it's safe."

"Three Ex-Marines against whatever trouble you have is more than enough," said one of the women coming out of the cabin. She was petite with lively green eyes, and she stepped up and held out her hand. "I'm Lily. Welcome to the Compound."

"And please don't let these two, or the name of this place, scare you."

The woman attached to that statement had pale blond straight hair that caused Shelby instant envy. She approached the still-scowling Zach, and Shelby noticed his face soften and the hard stare turn into something soft and full of love for the curvy little woman that tried to pass with her hand held out.

He didn't let her.

"Zacharias Steele," she scolded with a twinkle in her eye. "You let me greet Mike's guest properly."

"No." He kissed her nose as she stood looking up at him from the circle of his arms.

Shelby watched in wonder as the smile that spread across

his face transformed Zach from downright terrifying to loving husband with a mischievous side. And just like that, she relaxed. She should have trusted that Mike would never take her somewhere that wasn't completely safe.

"Get a room," Mike said to his friend as he tugged Shelby's hand, pulling her toward the cabin. "Let me show you my home."

Her eyes widened. "I thought you lived in Phoenix."

"I have a house there for work. But this is where I escape when city life is too much."

The interior could have been in a magazine. Not that the space was opulent like the place she was staying at, but because the design was simply beautiful. Large windows let in the light and showed off the woods in the back and front. The furniture was big and comfortable with a fireplace for cold nights. The kitchen was a gourmet dream. She'd forgotten Mike liked to cook. "I can see why you love it here." She looked at Mike and waved her free hand around. "This feels like a home."

"I hope you're hungry," he said. "The guys have been cooking most of the day, and the food is probably ready by now."

Shelby was shocked and amused. "Those two huge men did all the cooking?"

Mike grinned. "Yeah, Lily bakes, but Elizabeth tends to start fires when she tries to cook. Zach doesn't even let her near the microwave anymore. Besides, Jesse is an absolute whiz with a steak, and Zach is the master at smoking ribs."

Shelby's stomach rumbled at the mention of all the food. She let go of Mike's hand—she hadn't even realized she was still holding it—and moved to the back patio doors. Outside on the large deck she could see tables set up with a red-and-white-checkered cloth, pitchers of lemonade and iced tea.

Rebecca stood at the corral, petting a black-and-white Shetland pony that was clearly enjoying the attention.

Zach's son ran up and started pointing, and all four of the kids raced into the barn.

Shelby wasn't sure, but Rebecca looked like she was smiling. Her heart cracked at the sight. So many months had passed since Rebecca had smiled.

"She's in good hands," Mike said, coming to stand beside her. "Jesse tells me the cat had kittens so they're probably heading inside to check them out."

"It's been a long time since she's been around kids her age. We were so afraid she'd be taken away from us, either by the courts or if the father every showed up, that we kept her close." She turned from the patio and faced him. "This year has been crazy."

Mike put his hands on her shoulders and looked her in the eye. "We'll find some answers for you." He nodded toward the barn. "And for her."

"But it's not your problem. Why are you going through all this effort for us?"

Mike opened his mouth, but whatever he might have said was lost when Lily and Elizabeth came inside talking and laughing.

"We're just grabbing the coleslaw and salad from the fridge," Lily said. Then she winked at them both.

"Unless you'd like us to leave? It looked like we interrupted a moment," Elizabeth added with a grin.

Mike dropped his hands.

Shelby missed their warmth, but she conjured a smile for the ladies. "He was reassuring me. I'm a nervous wreck at the moment." She watched Mike turn and disappear outside. She wondered what he might have said. Shrugging away the thought, she pasted a smile on her face and went to help the two women talking so animatedly in the kitchen.

CHAPTER 10

"What's it like to be famous?" Lily asked.

Dinner was long over, and the kids were all inside, watching the latest animated movie. Shelby had seen more smiles out of Rebecca today than she'd seen all year long, and she had these wonderful people to thank. They'd made them both feel welcomed and part of the family. This was the first question about who Shelby was, and it didn't bother her in the least, because she could tell they were merely curious.

"It's one of the most amazing things. The money is great, but the loss of privacy is hard. Everyone seems to know what I'm doing before I do."

"Beth is famous," Zach said. His wife was snuggled up in his lap. "She's a writer."

"I'm not famous," she muttered.

Mike frowned as he came outside and took a seat next to Shelby on the porch swing. He stared at Zach and Elizabeth. "I have enough chairs for everyone, Beth."

She smiled and shrugged. "This is where he puts me."

Shelby hid a grin. "Do you write under a pen name?"

"She's Elizabeth Richardson," Zach said with pride.

Gasping, Shelby could feel her eyes widen. "I love your books. My best friend, Abby, is a rabid fan, and she would buy us both a copy of your book when the newest one was released."

Beth smiled, but Shelby could see a faint blush. The woman was a New York Times bestselling author for her last five books, and here she was in the backwoods of Arizona, snuggled up with her husband.

"Lily's a world-famous photo journalist," she said. It was like she was pushing the focus off of herself. "Her pictures broke open the Huerta cartel case five years ago."

"And almost got me killed in the process," Lily said.

Her husband wrapped an arm around her shoulders as they both smiled. "Thank God some devilishly handsome hero drove in to save the day," Jesse said with a straight face.

Zach and Mike groaned, and Elizabeth laughed out loud. Lily rolled her eyes and snorted, "He smelled like stale beer and sweat. Then he proceeded to have a shootout in the middle of a border town owned by that same drug cartel. I'm amazed we got out alive."

No wonder these people were so welcoming. Her life was nothing interesting compared to everyone here. She just stood on a stage and sang. She was about to say so when Mike's cell phone rang.

"Hanson," he said.

Shelby noticed Zach's and Jesse's body language changed very subtly. They were on alert as they waited to hear what was going on. Mike had already told her these men were his trusted friends, and they all helped out each other, without question, when needed. She was sure they were completely aware of her situation. Probably had more information than she did.

Mike wasn't giving much away, just listening and giving

an occasional grunt. Then he disconnected and looked at everyone. "We may have caught a break in the case."

Shelby let out a big sigh, thinking this was great news. "That's wonderful."

But Mike shook his head. "It's just another clue, and one that will still take time to track down. But it might be the one thing we have that will help us nail this guy. In the meantime, they haven't found the missing woman yet, and her disappearance is going on two days at this point."

"That poor woman," Beth said quietly.

Zach tightened his arms around her.

Lily shivered, and Jesse threw an arm around her. "I can't even imagine what she must be going through," she whispered.

"If she's even alive," Mike said.

The statement was stark and bare, but it's what they'd all been thinking. Crickets chirped in the sudden silence, as if a veil had dropped over the happy atmosphere of the night. The wonderful food she'd eaten churned in her stomach as the fissure of guilt cracked open just a little more. Shelby knew it wasn't her fault exactly, but in a way—it was, and nothing anyone could say would stop that feeling. Tara Schumway was likely being held and tortured because she looked like Shelby and fit into some twisted scheme of a psychopath.

"My new guy's got a real talent for this," Mike continued. "He and Casey are working hard on the case."

"Who's the new guy?" Jesse asked.

Shelby watched Mike's face change from deadly serious to a rather evil grin. And he glanced at Zach, who was playing with his wife's hair although, it was clear he was listening. She wondered what Mike was thinking because that grin was getting bigger.

"Daniel Wolfe," he said. "You remember him from your case, don't you, Beth?"

Shelby looked over and saw Beth's eyes widen about the time a bear growled. Except, the sound wasn't from a bear, it was Zach. "Of course, I remember Daniel. He took a bullet for me."

Jesse laughed and winked at Mike, who was still grinning broadly. "He took a bullet, because he was infatuated and rushed into the situation like some kind of rookie."

"He was a rookie to that kind of case," Mike said with a nod. "That was over five years ago."

"Time to go home," Zach said. Then he stood up with his wife in his arms. He frowned at his friends as they laughed at him.

"I *can* walk." But she wrapped her arms around her husband's neck and smiled.

Shelby covered her own smile and looked down at her hands. The big—still scary to her—guy had an enormous romantic and protective streak that he probably rarely showed to anyone except his wife. She was happy to see it, because it made her less wary of the solemn-faced man. And the carrying thing must be something that happened quite often because their son, Xavier, popped out of the house and said, "Time to go?"

"How did you know?" Mike joked.

The kid shrugged and smiled, "Dad always picks up Mom when he's ready to go home, otherwise Mom just keeps talking to Aunt Lily."

Zach shook his head and turned to leave, throwing a "keep me informed" look over his shoulder as his family left toward the front of the house, where the vehicles were parked.

"What was that about?" Shelby asked. Everyone was still smiling.

"Beth had a stalker problem about five years ago," Jesse said. "The situation was getting progressively more violent when she finally asked for help."

Mike joined in. "At the time, my detective was in burglary and was assigned to her case."

"And he was totally captivated with Beth," Lily added.

"Anyway," Mike said, "he happened to be from the same hometown as both Beth and Zach, and some other odd coincidences cast suspicion on him as the stalker. Needless to say, Zach is overly protective of his wife, and he still views Daniel with wariness."

"He doesn't like the way Daniel looks at Beth." Jesse laughed.

"That poor man is so intimidated by Zach he doesn't even talk to her," Lily said. "Unless, she corners him to say hi."

"Which only makes everything worse."

They all broke out into laughter. Nice to know she wasn't the only one who'd been through this kind of thing. Beth was such a sweet woman, that Shelby couldn't imagine someone trying to hurt her, or even wanting to. But that was the problem, there were sick people out there who didn't think like normal people. The constriction in her chest eased up just a tiny bit, but the stain of guilt was still there.

The patio door opened, and two sleepy-eyed girls came out and crawled up into their parent's laps. "We're ready to go home now. And Rebecca's sleeping on the couch—she didn't even make it to the end of the movie," they said in unison.

"Guess that's our cue," Lily said. "It was really nice meeting you, Shelby."

Shelby stood with Mike. "The pleasure was all mine, really. I never get to meet nice folks and just be a normal person for an evening. This was amazing."

"You should keep her, Uncle Mike."

"We like her, and she's pretty."

Shelby wasn't sure what to say to the twins who were looking at their "Uncle" as if keeping a woman was his choice. As for Mike, he looked like he swallowed a bullfrog. His friend Jesse threw his head back and laughed.

"I'll think about it, okay?" He finally choked out.

Lily winked at Shelby as she carried one of the girls and dragged her husband, who had the other twin, with her. "Good luck with that, Mike," she said as they rounded the corner.

When they were alone, Shelby shoved her hands in her jeans pockets and tried to contain her grin. Mike's dark complexion looked a bit darker around the ears, and she was deciding if it was actually a blush or not. The lights cast quite a few shadows, and when he finally looked at her, his expression was under control again. Too bad.

"Let me show you the bedrooms. It's late, and I'm sure you'd like to get to sleep."

Sleep was the last thing on her mind, but she accepted the suggestion. If nothing else, she wanted to get Rebecca settled in a room and under the covers. The night was chilly up here in the mountains. Shelby followed Mike inside.

He went straight to Rebecca, and scooped her up into his arms so smoothly that she never moved.

The sight melted her heart a little bit. He'd make a great father. *Whoa. That door is closed*, she thought to herself.

She tried to shy away from the idea of Mike with a houseful of kids, but the image circled back around her brain as she followed the big man holding her little girl so tenderly. He turned into a smaller room that was clearly a spare and laid Rebecca on the bed. Shelby moved to take off Rebecca's shoes and tuck her in, placing a kiss on her pert little nose.

They left the room, cracking the door slightly so Rebecca

didn't get scared in the middle of the night. Not that she normally woke up. That girl slept the sleep of the innocent.

"Let me show you to your room."

The room was big, masculine, and clearly the master. "But this is your room," Shelby said.

"The room is closest to Rebecca's, and I thought you'd want to be nearby in case she needs you. I'll be fine in the other guest room." He pointed down a short hallway. "The one on the left." He nodded toward the room. "The wives left your bags and things they bought for you both inside."

What a sweet thing to do. "I really love your friends, Mike."

"I do too." He said it simply, and then turned and walked down the hall.

HE WASN'T sure what woke him, but Mike was instantly alert. He lay still and looked up into the corner of the ceiling. There, a small black sensor showed a steady green light. His alarm was courtesy of Zach and Jesse, who were the best in the home and business protection industry. If there was a perimeter problem, the light would flash blue. And if there was a breach to the home itself, it would flash red. Green meant everything was good.

He slowed down his breathing, getting his body under control. Mike had been in the middle of an intensely erotic dream involving his houseguest, and if he jackknifed out of bed, he was afraid he'd injure himself.

Listening hard, he heard something coming from the front of the house. After sliding out of bed, he slipped into his jeans, grabbed the gun that was on the nightstand, and padded out of his room. No alarm was full proof, and he didn't take chances.

The door to Shelby's room was closed, but a quick peek inside Rebecca's room showed the girl was still asleep.

Soundlessly, he moved down the hallway. His gun was down by his leg, but he was fast enough to bring it up if he found an actual problem. Coming out of the hall, what he found was a problem, but of an entirely different kind. And his body went into overdrive.

Damn.

Shelby sat on the wood floor, haloed by the moonlight streaming through the back patio door. She was using that light to write notes on the many pieces of paper surrounding her crossed legs.

Her very bare, crossed legs.

She wore one of his old blue flannel shirts, the tails riding up her thighs and the too-long sleeves rolled and cuffed at her wrists. The hair that she hated so much was a tangled riot of gold around her face. It obscured her expression from him, but not her voice. She was singing.

The tune was something new, because he knew all her songs word for word, and he'd never heard this one before. But for some reason, it sounded somewhat familiar. He slid the gun into his jeans at the small of his back and leaned against the wall. He was afraid she'd stop if she knew he was there, and he just wanted to look at her. Jesus, he missed this woman.

Shelby hummed the tune that only she could hear in her head, as she made notes. Then she started to sing.

It was quiet, but her voice was pure magic, wrapping around him and sending him straight back to the old days when she would take over his bed with her guitar and notes and write music.

The last note ended softly. "I always did write my best stuff at your place."

Since she knew he was there, he moved closer and took

up a position on her right side. He wanted to see her face, and she looked so beautiful sitting in the moonlight that he was half afraid she was a fairy, her wings hidden until she flew away. "I was just thinking that tonight was like the old days. Me waking up in the middle of the night with you singing and writing."

"I'm still a night owl, and I do my best stuff when everyone else is sleeping."

"I would imagine that being an entertainer keeps you up and out 'til all hours of the day and night as well."

Shelby shrugged and finally looked up at him. Her blue eyes were luminescent in the pale light. "I could say the same about you. Homicide isn't exactly a nine-to-five kind of job."

Mike gave a faint smile. "I sometimes wonder why I even bother to sleep."

Shelby laughed lightly.

Mike's gaze was drawn down from her face. His shirt was misbuttoned, as if she'd been in such a hurry to leave her room that she couldn't be bothered to button the shirt correctly. And he was glad, because he got an incredible view of her cleavage. No bra. Which made him wonder if she wore any panties.

Calm down, Marine.

He had to give himself a pep talk or his body would go off like a damned teenager with his first crush. When he pulled his gaze from the tantalizing sight of her body, he found himself the focus of an intense once-over. And he felt her eyes like an actual caress.

His jeans became uncomfortably tight as her gaze seared the muscles of his chest and arms. Mike enjoyed the way she looked at him. He was proud of his body, he used it like the machine it was; to fight and win against whatever obstacles might be in his way.

Right now, the obstacle was that damn shirt.

But he wasn't sure he even wanted to fight or win, even though the sexual tension was thick.

She reached up to push the hair off her forehead, pulling his shirt tight across her breasts.

She had to be doing that on purpose, but he couldn't pull his gaze off the intriguing gap the strained buttons made. And when she focused on the bulge in his pants and bit her full bottom lip, he almost lunged. But doing that would plunge him into a rabbit hole big enough to swallow his soul, which was still scarred from the first time around.

"What do you think of my new song?" Her voice was husky, but she stayed still on the floor.

"It's a hit."

"It will be—for someone else."

Mike frowned as he considered her words. "Why wouldn't you keep that one for yourself? It's beautiful."

"I'm getting out of the business," she said it quietly. "That's why these concerts are so important and why I have to be there. A lot of money is on the line. Enough that I can retire and take care of Rebecca. I want her to have a normal life. Being on the road with me isn't good for her. She needs stability and a set of friends that she's not scared she'll lose if she goes on the road for a year or more."

He heard what she said, but something else was bothering him. Why did he suddenly remember the words? "That song. It's the one the killer stuffed into the hairdresser's bag, isn't it?"

When he saw her nod, he felt like everything clicked into place. He'd been missing a piece of the puzzle and that was motive. Shelby thought it was something to do with Rebecca but it wasn't. And the stalking wasn't a weird fetish for this guy. Somehow, he'd been close enough to know that she was quitting the music business. "Who knows that you're done after this set of concerts?"

Shelby got to her feet slowly, staring as she cocked her head to the side. "What are you thinking?"

"Who knows, Shelby?"

"Madge, my agent, the band, and my road crew. I couldn't just leave them hanging with no jobs after this. But everyone has been sworn to secrecy. I'm announcing my retirement at the end of the third concert."

"Somehow this guy knows. This is the secret that triggered him. And he's trying to make you understand that you have to keep singing. That's why the crime scenes are staged the way they are. He's recreating your biggest hits. And the fact that they're all love songs probably has something to do with his fixation."

"He thinks I'm singing to him, doesn't he?"

Mike heard the revulsion in her voice, but she was right. "He's deluded and crazy, but yes, I'm sure that's exactly what he thinks."

She shivered and hugged herself as she looked away and out the window. "All I ever wanted to do was sing and write songs."

"And be famous."

That produced a small smile. "True."

"I think you've achieved that, many times over."

Shelby turned back to Mike and shrugged. "My career been a lot of work with moments of sheer awesomeness. But no one ever realizes how tired I am, all the time. Or how many times my voice has been so overworked that I lose it for a week or so."

"Or how lonely you are?"

She nodded. "Or that. The fans all think I have this amazing life that's nothing but parties and glittering clothes. But I go to bed alone or sometimes I sneak in with Rebecca, because I can hold her close."

"You chose to walk away from everything you knew, into that world."

"I know." She looked him over and took a step closer. "Sometimes I regret that choice."

Mike stayed where he was, but part of him felt like running. She was too close, smelled too good and looked too damned sexy for his piece of mind. His jaw clenched, but he stood his ground. "What do you want from me?"

"A kiss, to start. One that isn't filled with anger and regret."

She stalked him in the moonlight, seductive without even trying.

She reached out and touched his stomach, which contracted at the light contact. "You make me feel things I thought were long buried."

Mike sucked in a breath. "This isn't a good idea, Shelby Lynn." He used her stage name in a sad attempt to keep her at bay. But she just smiled, as if she knew he was desperate.

"I think it's a very good idea, Detective."

She pressed her body against his, her palms on his pecs, shaping the muscles and setting fire to his bloodstream.

"You brought me here to protect me. and right now I'm in danger."

"Yeah?"

"Yeah," she whispered, "I'll die if you don't kiss me, now."

His body took over then, telling his brain to shut the hell up. She was in his arms, and he had her up on her tip-toes as his lips took hers. The years fell away, and she was his again, strong, passionate Shelby, who never shied away from telling him exactly what she wanted.

And what she wanted was this kiss.

CHAPTER 11

S helby's whole body shuddered as Mike plundered her mouth. His tongue slipped inside and turned her inside out. She pressed up against his gorgeous body, and there was no doubt in her mind that he wanted her as much as she wanted him. "I've missed you," she said when she could.

"No, you didn't," he growled back at her.

He might never forgive her, but Shelby couldn't bring herself to be upset about it at this moment. Right now, all she cared about was that he was holding her and kissing her as if she was the only woman in the world.

He made her feel alive. A real, live, red-blooded woman that was wanted by a man. Wanted because she was a woman, not just a famous face.

She ran her hands up into his hair and scraped her nails along his scalp. It used to drive him wild, and she wanted him wild. Shelby knew that if he had time to think, he'd pull away. There was no way she wanted that, what she wanted was him. Hot and raw and inside her, making her forget everything but what they used to be together.

"Damn it. What're you doing to me?"

Mike's voice was ragged, and she couldn't catch her breath enough to answer. So she nipped his chin and tugged at his hair, pulling his mouth back to hers. She rubbed her body against his, feeling his erection against her soft belly. "I want you."

He kissed her again, more out of control this time, picking her up and turning. He set her on the kitchen counter, putting himself between her legs. His hands were on her bare skin at her hips, touching her.

"No panties," he breathed out.

"I never wear any to bed."

His hands flexed on her skin, but didn't move.

Shelby's palms roamed his shoulders and down his biceps, feeling the power there. He could so easily crush her with those massive arms, but he'd never been anything but gentle , even when he was young.

His body was rigid, and he moved his hands from her hips. "Shelby—"

"Just kiss me."

And he did, as if he couldn't get enough of her. She took control this time, sucking his full bottom lip and biting him gently. Hooking her ankles around his waist, she pulled him closer, pressing his hardness against her straining body. She was more than ready for him. One quick flick of his zipper, and he could be inside her.

Shelby dove for the little strip of metal that separated her from heaven.

But he trapped her hands. "I don't think—" But whatever he was about to say was lost as a door opened and closed, and Mike's head whipped toward the sound.

Shelby also turned toward the hallway and saw the light to the bathroom shone under the bottom of the door. She sighed. Rebecca was awake. She looked at Mike, who was back to being the detective she didn't know very well, instead of the passionate man she had in her arms just a few seconds ago. "I better go and check on her."

Mike nodded and then helped her down from the counter, letting go of her immediately once her feet were on the floor again. Then he moved around her and into the kitchen.

That's when she noticed the gun handle sticking out of the back of his jeans. "You always have a gun on you in the middle of the night?"

He looked back with his eyebrow raised. "I do when I'm protecting stubborn women and innocent children."

She put her hands on her hips, the banter helping to calm her racing heart and out-of-control libido. "So you've had a parade of women up here then?"

But he didn't play back. He filled a couple of glasses with water and came back to hand her one. "My experience has been that kids get thirsty in the middle of the night."

Then he downed his own glass of water, and Shelby watched his throat work like a fascinated school girl. She shook herself out of it and held up the water in thanks. "You think of everything."

"You should get some sleep," he said.

Seemed like everyone in her life was always telling her that. But, she was tired. "You were about to stop just now, weren't you?" She stared up into his eyes. "Before Rebecca went to the bathroom?"

He nodded, and then reached out to snag one of her curls. He pulled it lightly and watched it spring back into shape. "You and me—"

"Not a good idea, is it?" Boy, did her body disagree. And maybe the cold lump of tissue called her heart did too.

"I need to focus on catching this guy. My job is to protect you and Rebecca, and I can't afford to be distracted."

"And, I'm just a distraction?" She couldn't help the sharp slap of disappointment, but she also understood she couldn't expect Mike to ignore their history and pick up where they left off all those years ago. Her big bad Marine was running. Shelby had hurt him in the deepest way a person could be hurt. She had a long way to go to heal that, but she was determined to try. She'd seen a glimpse of what life could be like, and she wanted it. Wanted it with all her heart. Wanted him. "Thanks for the water," she said softly. "And for everything you're doing for us."

She turned to go and take Rebecca back to bed, because the little girl was watching them from the darkened hallway, bright eyes inquisitive. When she went to her room a little while later, Shelby saw his door was closed.

She decided to ignore the finality of that. There would be another opportunity in the next couple of days to change his mind. She hadn't picked Phoenix to retire just because it was her home town. She'd lied when she'd told him she hadn't looked into his past. Not that she'd read the report Madge had on him. She hadn't had to read past the initial page. The word—single—had been all she was looking for.

The truth was, she'd been wishing on a star when she chose to come back home. She wished with all her heart that the man she'd left behind might still harbor some feelings for her, the way she did for him. For a while now, she'd been lying to herself, thinking she'd never see him again. That the past was over. But she was a horrible liar. The possibility had always been in the back of her mind that she'd make sure to run into him. She had to.

Shelby Lynn might have loved the spotlight and the fame, but plain and simple Shelby Collins had never stopped loving Mike Hanson.

〜

SHE'S NOT EVEN THERE. I told you she doesn't know you exist.

"Where is she?" He strained his eyes but the room she stayed in was clean and devoid of movement. Two days had passed since he'd seen her, and he was taking a chance coming here during the daytime. "I know she watched the videos."

Maybe that big bitch she lives with wouldn't let her watch.

"But—"

STOP WHINING!

Slapping his head, he said, "Don't yell at me. It hurts."

Too bad. Stop being a pussy and get back to work. Shelby will return and then you can do whatever you want.

"I need to know where she is. What if she never comes back? What if—"

But he couldn't finish because his vision started blurring and he knew he was losing control. The shadow inside was fighting to come out, and it was winning. He gave his head a hard slap, but it was too late. He'd been so focused on where Shelby had gone that he hadn't been vigilant enough.

As he slid backward, he felt the rock and gravel dig into his back. He was on the side of the mountain again, looking down into Shelby's room. But he wouldn't wake up there. He never remembered what happened when the Shadow Man took over, but the outcome was always bad. Sometimes it was even worse than he could imagine.

MIKE HAD BEEN DOING some fancy maneuvering, and with the help of his friends, he'd avoided being alone with Shelby since the incident in the moonlight two days before. Even if he felt like a damned fool, he knew his weaknesses, and Shelby was number one on the list. He was falling under her spell. Giving in was not an option, but sleeping with an eternal hard-on was really fucking uncomfortable.

At this point, he was afraid to leave his room in the middle of the night. He'd lain awake for hours, listening to the house and any movements within last night. Convinced everyone was asleep, he'd crept out for a beer. Mike figured he'd watch TV and drink a single adult beverage for relaxation. Just one beer was all he'd wanted. But Shelby had been there ahead of him, in little more than a couple strips of lace that had tied his tongue and made the situation in his pants so much worse. He'd hobbled back to his room and an ice-cold shower before she'd even had a chance to get up off the couch.

Now he stood in his office, watching everyone have fun outside. The kids were playing with the kittens again, this time right outside the barn doors in the sunlight. Mama kitty stretched out in the sun, while the kids had the kittens bouncing around, chasing string. Zach and Jesse were cutting wood, each trying to out-do the other with single chops to split each piece. The women were having fun yelling encouragement or groaning when the log didn't split open the first time.

Mike was hiding. Again. The relief he felt when his cell went off was ridiculous. Finally, something to do besides stare at Shelby. "Hanson," he answered. And if his tone was abrupt, it was too fucking bad.

"Whoa, who pissed in your Wheaties?" Damon Dupree said.

"No one." Mike tried to interject some humor into his voice, but failed. "Sorry, buddy. I'm on edge with this case."

"That's understandable, because this case just got a whole lot weirder."

Mike had known Damon would come up with something. His friend was smart and resourceful. And so was his wife. "Whatcha got?"

"Two mysteries, not one."

"That's all I need." He moved away from the window, sat in his chair, and rubbed a hand over his tired face. Then he pulled out a pen and notebook.

"Sorry, man. That detective Shelby Lynn hired was a high-priced hack. His office was fancy, but the guy specializes in cheating spouses, not missing persons. Dani got up in his face and read him the riot act for taking money he hadn't earned and not doing a goddamn thing that was useful."

"Nice. I bet that was a sight." Mike shook his head. He wondered why Madge hadn't handled the investigating with her normal efficiency, but then decided Shelby had likely handled that aspect of it herself. Due to her guilt.

"I love that woman," Damon said. "What info do you want first?"

"Tell me about Abby."

"She was good at hiding her end of the relationship, but her douche-bag boyfriend wasn't as careful. His name's Charles Weston. We learned he was a small time musician who did minor gigs pretty much everywhere. He worked with a few in-studio house bands, but he and Abby met when he was hired by Shelby's opening act. He was on the tour for almost a year, off and on. For him, that was the 'big time.'"

"He was just part of the crowd, that's why no one saw them together. Or why no one really noticed."

"Exactly," Damon replied. "But the guy we talked to says he was always bragging Abby was just a stepping stone. He wanted an introduction to Shelby Lynn."

"Damn. I'm not telling her that part," Mike said. "Were you able to locate him?" Because that type of guy could easily turn into the kind of stalker that went violent. And if what

Shelby told him was true about Abby's bruises, then he was already a violent man.

"Yeah."

Mike heard the pause. That wasn't a good sign. "And?"

"And he's dead. That's the second mystery."

"I'm guessing his death wasn't an accident or something simple then?"

"No, and this is where the case gets odd. At first the local PD thought it was a robbery, because clear evidence showed his wallet and all his money were taken. He was found alone in his studio apartment, with no signs of forced entry. But enough takeout remained to make them believe that whoever killed this guy stuck around for a couple of weeks with the body."

Mike dropped his head and rubbed his neck. This whole situation was getting stranger. "Do they have any leads?"

"Not a single one."

Mike cocked his head to the side. "What haven't you told me?"

"Charles Weston has been dead exactly one year."

"The same time Abby went missing," Mike said. "What did the police say about that?"

"They can't tie Charles to Abby by as much as a carpet fiber. *If* he was living in this apartment when they were together, then she never set foot in the place."

"They don't know how long he was living there?"

Damon sighed. "The place is an old textile warehouse that was turned into studio apartments. The landlord is shady as hell. He's cash only and keeps lousy records. He said Charles had been there a number of years, but he couldn't give an exact time. I'm going out there today to check out the place and nose around a little."

"And nothing new on Abby?"

"I have feelers out to a few other departments in the

outlying areas for any Jane Does, since nothing came up around Nashville. I figure her body was dumped a lot farther out."

"Sorry to drag you into all this, but everything you've found really helps."

"Hey, man, I owed you. Besides, Dani's having a little too much fun playing detective. She's good at it, though, or maybe it's all that red hair and big green eyes. It's amazing the way everyone just opens up and starts answering all her questions."

"Are you still coming out for the concert?"

"We'll be there, and I'll be ready."

"Alright." Mike would have to find Damon a nest at the concert, somewhere up high enough that he could see the whole arena. The logistics of sneaking him and his sniper rifle inside would be a nightmare, but Mike would get the task handled. "Call me if you find out anything else."

"You got it." Damon disconnected.

Mike slowly put down his cell. Now what? Someone else was involved, but who he was, and how, was unclear. Two mysteries.

Shit.

He would have to call in all the favors owed. Not that the guys would look at his request that way. When a Marine needed help, his brothers would always be there. That was their way. Their code.

Right or wrong, he would protect Shelby during her shows any way he could. And while he trusted his brothers in blue to handle most of the regular security, they weren't as good as his friends.

The late morning had turned into afternoon, and it was time for lunch. He couldn't hide much longer. Either Beth or Lily would come drag him out. Or worse, Shelby would come for him which ran the risk of being alone together.

Alone with a desirable woman. One he knew intimately. How she tasted, how she smelled. How she moaned when she came.

Damn.

He adjusted his jeans when he stood and strode outside.

Time to join in and show Zach and Jesse how to chop wood. The work and axe would keep his mind off a certain sexy singer. Yeah right. He'll be lucky if he doesn't sever his own leg.

CHAPTER 12

*S*helby wasn't sure how he did it, but Mike had tactfully avoided being alone with her for two days. She was getting a complex about it.

"Good God, those are some handsome guys," Lily said. "I'd bring out my camera, but then they'll just get worse with their antics."

"That's true," Beth chimed in, "but they might take off their shirts."

She sounded so hopeful that Shelby laughed.

The two women leered at their husbands from the shade of the porch while drinking homemade lemonade.

Shelby was privately jealous of the obvious love she saw between the couples. They were openly affectionate with one another, as well as all the kids. "I wouldn't mind seeing Mike with his shirt off again."

That brought Beth's head around and her eyes widened. "Again?"

Lily grinned. "Do tell."

"Nothing to tell." Shelby sighed, making it properly dramatic, and she fought a laugh. She hadn't had this much fun talking with anyone since Abby. She pushed away the pang thinking of her friend inevitably brought, and instead focused on the smiling women in front of her. "Hard not to see something when you're living with a man, even temporarily."

Lily and Beth shared a look.

Beth grinned and winked, "Have you noticed the shower is big enough for two?"

Shaking her head, Lily reached out and put her hand on Shelby's. "Beth's obsessed with the showers. All three houses were built by the same contractor, and he apparently thought the guys needed showers big enough to do aerobics in."

"Hmmm, aerobics," Beth said with a lascivious smile.

Shelby shook her head. "You *have* been married for a while, right?"

"Over six years now."

Lily threw back her head and laughed. "You do remember what she writes, don't you? Zach is her willing victim every time she wants to "work out" a scene."

Shelby covered her face, "Now I won't be able to read those scenes without thinking of you and Zach."

"The downside of knowing the author." Lily sympathized. "I can't read them either, not anymore. But I have all my signed copies sitting on my bookcase."

"Speaking of signed copies," Beth said. "We'd love it if you signed a couple of our CDs."

"Only if you sign my copies of your books when you come for the concert. And I know I have an Arizona Highways magazine around somewhere in the house in town, Lily. I'd love to have your signature as well. You take amazing pictures."

"Aren't we just a talented group?" Beth said, but she eyed her husband as he shoved Mike.

"Can I confess something?" Shelby asked.

The women looked at her with bright glances and raised eyebrows.

"Mike and I were a thing when we were younger." She waved her hand in a circle. "Before all the fame. But I'm guessing you might know that already."

Lily nodded. "We knew and were kind of hoping you being here was a good sign."

"Mike never brings anyone home," Beth said.

It warmed her heart to hear it, even though Mike told her that. And she had a feeling these ladies would be on her side with her request. "I have a rather rude request, then."

Beth grinned. "You'd like us to take our kids and husbands and leave?"

Shelby returned the smile and nodded. "Am I horrible?"

"Not at all," Lily said. "Sometimes you have to smack them over the head to get them to your way of thinking. And Mike is exceptionally hard-headed." She stood and stretched. "We'll be out of here as soon as lunch is over."

"Which is now. Shelby, why don't you call in the kids and have them wash up, and we'll start laying out the food," Beth said. "Then we'll drag our brood home." She winked and went inside the cabin.

Shelby really liked Beth and Lily. They were so nice and understanding and genuinely cared about Mike. He didn't have many friends growing up, and now he had a core group that would lay down their lives for him, just the way he would for them.

That kind of rapport was something she wanted. She and Abby had it and she missed it. But she had Rebecca and Madge. And while she truly liked her band and crew—that was work. This was family.

And home.

⌁

After lunch, Shelby lost track of Mike and Rebecca. The same thing happened a couple of times yesterday as well. She'd see Mike bend down and talk to the little girl then he'd hold out his hand. Rebecca, who was normally shy, slipped her hand into his large one with no hesitation and they disappeared together. Shelby wanted them to like each other, so she'd left them alone. She worked on her music or napped, since she still wasn't sleeping much at night.

Today, she was curious.

Just the three of them were here now, and Shelby decided to follow Mike and Rebecca to discover what was going on. Rounding the enormous barn, she saw a round corral with the little Shetland pony saddled up and waiting.

Mike stood, pointing to the various pieces of tack the horse wore and explaining what each one was. He and Rebecca stood side by side inside the pen.

Shelby pulled back into the shadows and watched. She and Abby had been on the road for as long as Rebecca had been alive, so there hadn't been time to find horseback riding lessons. Even when Rebecca had begged for months to learn how to ride. The pang in her heart reminded Shelby this was why she couldn't cancel those concerts. She needed to give Rebecca everything she'd missed out on in the past seven years.

"I know you don't like to talk much, but Cinnamon here likes to obey commands with noises and by voice," Mike said before making a clicking noise out of the side of his mouth.

The horse's ears perked up at the sound.

"See? Now she's waiting for a command. Can you make the same noise?"

Shelby held her breath—hoping.

Rebecca reached out and touched Cinnamon's neck. Then she looked up at Mike.

He repeated the clicks.

Then Rebecca looked back at the horse and tried. The sounds came out softly, but they were there. Three little clicks that matched Mike's almost perfectly.

"That's exactly right, Rebecca. See how her ears flicked back toward you?" He waited until she nodded and then continued. "Now when you want her to go from a walk to a trot, you'll kick her flanks gently and make that noise. And when you want her to stop, you have to pull back on the reins and say, 'Whoa'."

"Whoa," her little voice echoed.

Shelby had both hands covering her mouth to keep quiet. She didn't want to disturb the moment by doing something stupid like bursting into tears. Instead, she tore her tear-laden gaze away from Rebecca to look at the man who had her daughter talking. He was big and could be intimidating, and a tough-as-nails former Marine, but to her, he was a miracle.

Her heart felt like it might burst with all the emotions she had. The fear Rebecca would never speak again, the undying hope her best friend was still alive, and the love had never gone away, that was bursting through her for the man she left behind. And that was it, the real reason she'd chosen to come home to retire. She could have gone anywhere, but Shelby had been determined to return to Phoenix. The reason was clear now, in a way that she'd never have admitted to before.

She loved Mike and she wanted him back. And, this time, she was determined keep him.

Backing away, she retraced her steps to the cabin and let her man and her child have the moment of triumph. But, in the end, the moment was hers because she had a goal. Not like the one that led her to Nashville in the first place. Fame was temporary in this fickle world. This one was for the rest of her life, and this dream was the only one that truly mattered.

Love. Family. Home.

And she would fight for them.

HE WOKE UP, not sure where he was. But his head hurt so bad, the ache made him stay still until the pain dulled to a throb. "What did you do, Charlie?" he whispered. He thought he tasted blood.

But Charlie was quiet, because he was a shadow.

Looking around, he wasn't sure where he was at first. He didn't even know what time it was, but he felt sticky. Like something foreign was on his body, but he couldn't figure out what. It was dark, so he moved slowly and sat up. He lay on a hard floor that wasn't smooth and felt like concrete. Maybe he was in one of the secret places.

When he didn't feel as if he might vomit, he got to his feet. His head protested, but he stood still, holding onto what felt like a table until the pain receded again. That was better. And his eyes were adjusting. The room wasn't pitch-black after all. Light streamed in through the high windows. He was in a bathroom of sorts, with a couple of industrial sinks and a commode in the corner.

"Where did you bring me?" he asked, but knew there wouldn't be an answer. The shadow normally rested after he took over for an extended amount of time. Especially, when he was mad.

And Charlie was always mad.

Leaving the room, he walked out into the wide open space of the main warehouse, and that's when he knew that Charlie had been in a rage. The carnage in front of him wasn't what he had planned. He'd been having so much fun with the woman. With his newest Shelby Lynn.

But that was now over.

He walked around and looked at what had been done. He could do nothing now—not for her. She was supposed to be the pinnacle in his video montage, but she wouldn't make the cut. He shrugged. What a waste.

Turning away, he found the lantern he used to light up his work space. He still didn't feel right. Going back into the room with the sinks and the small table, he flipped on the lantern and turned back to the mirror that was partially intact on the wall. The bottom half had been vandalized at some point, but one whole side was unbroken.

So much blood.

The face that stared back wasn't his any longer. The creature in the mirror was something else. Something reptilian that slithered into the small spaces. Bringing a hand to his face, he saw that it too was covered in blood. So much that the smell suddenly overwhelmed him. "Who are you?"

I'm you, a voice hissed back.

It was the Shadow. He wasn't resting after all.

It was Charlie.

He didn't even exist anymore.

DANIEL PUSHED BACK from his desk in frustration. He wished he were making more headway, but every rodent specialty store came up empty. The only chinchillas sold recently were to a little Hawaiian girl who'd promptly named them after a Disney movie that was set on her home island. Her parents had been surprised, yet helpful, when he'd shown up at the door to ask about the purchase.

When his cell rang, he hoped the news was something

good because he wasn't getting anywhere and it was pissing him off. "Wolfe," he barked.

"Peter and the . . . " Her voice trailed off.

That threw him for a moment, "What?"

"Now I have the music from that story running through my head. Oh well, guess it's better than Shelby Lynn's stuff. I'm suddenly addicted. And I don't normally listen to country music, but that chick's got the pipes."

"Casey?" he asked, but he already knew. She was like a sudden storm after his gloomy afternoon. Her breezy attitude blew him off course, but he couldn't be too upset. He liked her voice.

"Who else? I have some good news."

"I could use it." And he could. Something was better than the nothing he had.

"Victim number one has a name, finally."

He pulled a pen out from under the papers strewn across his desk. "Okay, shoot."

"Name is Priscilla Trenton, she's twenty-three, single, and is a missing person from Nashville, Tennessee. I'm thinking that's not a coincidence, and that her folks were clearly influence by the proximity to Graceland."

Daniel sat back in his chair. "No, I don't think that it is," he said slowly. "I've been having some doubts about this guy being home grown. So what if he's not?"

"Time of death is roughly the same day Shelby Lynn said she got into town."

"Son of a bitch. He brought victim one with him. He wasn't hunting here, he was hunting in Nashville." What the hell happened in Nashville to start all this?

"I'm already trying to match prints and dentals for victim number two in Nashville, just in case he brought two bodies."

While he didn't think victim number two would be from the same place, he did wonder about the chinchillas. They were small and easy to move. What if he hadn't bought them here, but already had them?

"Keep checking locally, as well as the route from Nashville to here. He could have picked up the second girl from the road."

"Thanks for the tip, Captain Obvious."

He could hear the sarcasm dripping through the phone. "Not that you aren't already doing that, I meant."

"I'm telling Mike to fire you when I talk to him, due to your lack of people skills."

He snorted. "I have people skills."

"First, you think I'm a hooker, and now you think I'm an idiot. That is not winning me over."

He took a moment to picture her in that dress and those heels. And he tried to keep the smile out of his voice. "I don't think you're an idiot, and I never said you were a hooker."

"You didn't have to, Daniel," she said his name with a bit of extra sweetness.

"Mike's not firing me." He laughed. He enjoyed her spicy wit that livened up his bad day.

"He likes me better than you."

He imagined her sticking out her tongue at the phone. *Hmmm*, what he could do with that tongue. Then he shook himself out of that image, because he didn't want to think about the little medical examiner that way. That idea was too complicated. But, he didn't stop baiting her. "That's because you show up to crime scenes looking like a hooker." He hung up. Let her chew on that. Then he laughed out loud as he pictured the look of outrage on her face.

He turned back to his computer, determined to find those freaking chinchillas. That hair was the only clue this bastard had left behind, and Daniel wanted to nail his ass to the wall with it.

CHAPTER 13

*H*e'd been a little worried when all his friends suddenly had something to do after lunch, and Mike suspected a little matchmaking from Beth and Lily. They really liked Shelby and had been worried about him being alone for some time now. But what he enjoyed most was watching his bad-ass Marine brothers get dragged home by their little wives. The apology for not backing him up was written on their faces, but the shrugs and sheepish grins told the story. The sight was worth the abandonment.

Or so he thought.

He hadn't counted on Shelby's determination. Or Rebecca's sweetness. Both just about brought him to his knees.

Spending the afternoon teaching Rebecca how to ride had been more enjoyable than he could have imagined. That she was talking was its own reward. He just hoped she would stay open and talkative and not retreat back into her silent world.

Mike had worried about Shelby and how she would take Rebecca suddenly talking again after a year, but he decided that she'd be fine. Now he stood, making dinner for the girls and all he had to do was ask Rebecca to tell him what her favorite part of the day was.

"Riding Cinnamon was the best part."

"Why don't you tell your Aunt Shelby about it?"

And she turned and did just that. Rebecca had been silent so long that the words just rushed out in long streams.

Mike watched Shelby surreptitiously, but she smiled and laughed with the little girl as if no time had passed in silence. And if her eyes were shinier than normal, he thought she did a great job of holding the emotion in.

Dinner was simple, but the company was amazing. Mike felt something move inside as he listened to the girls chatter. They included him as well, both reaching over to touch him. Rebecca in excitement as she talked about owning a horse of her own someday, and she wanted the exact same horse as Cinnamon. Shelby's touch was absent minded, as if it was normal to reach out to him and squeeze his hand while Rebecca talked.

It was almost like having a preview of what his life could have been. If things had been different, and Shelby hadn't left him all those years ago. Rebecca could be their child, and none of the heartache would have happened because he would have been there to protect her.

He got to his feet and grabbed the dishes, jerking them from the table. Anger welled up inside of him. Anger with himself and with Shelby. Her single-minded dreams had robbed them both of this, and he still couldn't get over it.

"I can get that," she said.

He shook his head. "Why don't you go tuck Rebecca into bed? The drive back to town tomorrow is long, and I want to be in place before you have to be at the concert venue for the sound checks and rehearsal." At the sink, he braced his hands on the counter, and he was glad he did because two little arms went around his legs, giving him a big hug.

"I want you to tuck me in, Mike."

The demand was one he couldn't refuse. As much as he wanted to distance himself from them both, he just couldn't. Big blue eyes dominated her serious face. No way could he do anything to disappoint this little girl. Ever.

"I guess you deserve one last ride tonight." He bent down, and she climbed on his back as if she'd been doing it her whole life. With a loud whinny and nicker, he cantered off toward her room, her giggles the best music in the world. He passed Shelby and she turned slightly away from them, but not before he saw the tears streaking down her face.

Damn, he hadn't meant to make her cry. He thought she'd be happy Rebecca was finally talking, and she probably was. Women cried at the oddest stuff. He'd witnessed the behavior over the years with Beth and Lily, and he was always amazed at how the guys handled it without losing their cool. But they never seemed to mind.

The women he normally had contact with were all police personnel or Casey. And he couldn't imagine anything other than being shot making those ladies cry. Maybe not even then. He could picture Casey cussing while simultaneously telling everyone around her how to process the evidence correctly.

They tucked in Rebecca, and Mike left the girls alone to catch up with whatever girlie stuff that a mother and daughter normally did. Even if Rebecca called Shelby her Aunt, it was a mother/daughter type of relationship they had.

He washed the few dishes they used and then went outside. Checking the perimeter was always a nightly ritual, even when a psychopath wasn't on the loose. It was calming to walk in the woods, breathe in the fresh mountain air, and listen to a night devoid of all the city sounds. He took his time because he didn't know when he'd be able to get back. This interlude had been more about safety than pleasure, although spending so much time with his friends and their families was always amazing.

When he walked back into the house, he saw the lights were off and all the bedroom doors were closed. Part of him was disappointed Shelby wasn't in some flimsy bit of nothing, lying in wait. But a bigger part of him was just relieved. His resistance to that woman was dangerously low.

Mike checked the windows and doors and made sure the alarm was set, before heading down the hall to his bedroom. A nice, long, hot shower sounded good, even if it normally ended up ice cold, due to his over-heated imagination.

He stayed in the shower longer than normal and when he stepped into his bedroom, he knew he wasn't alone. His body knew it as well, and all that cold water didn't mean a damn thing the minute she dropped her robe.

"Shelby—"

Her name was a plea. A groan. A prayer.

"I want you, Mike. So much."

She moved like a dancer, gracefully gliding toward him and stopping with only a breath between their naked bodies.

"Please don't make me leave." She reached for him.

He cursed and caught her wrists in a light grip, keeping those nimble fingers away from his body. If she touched him, it was over and he knew this was a mistake. "We can't." He gritted his teeth. "I can't."

"Why are you afraid of this? Of me?"

Her gaze implored him, and then she pressed her warm soft body to his. The willpower he was holding onto so tightly cracked—which such force that he was surprised jolt didn't rip him in two.

"Please," she whispered.

"What you do to me," he mumbled before he let go of her

wrists. Willpower be damned. She was there in his arms and kissing him back as fiercely as he kissed her. The tidal wave of emotion and feeling he'd kept in check rushed over him and carried them both away.

Good idea, bad idea—it didn't matter anymore. Mike was done thinking. His body was in control. The woman he'd never gotten over was naked and wanting in his arms. No way he could refuse her and survive. And if she walked away again, he'd figure out how to live without her. He'd have to.

"You do the same thing to me," she said.

Her hands roamed his body. Light butterfly touches that burned and branded his skin. She brushed those fingers over his chin, down his neck, shaping the muscles on his chest. He was hard and ready, but at the touch of her nails raking lightly down his stomach, he thought he would explode. He could not handle her touching him any longer until he calmed down.

He picked her up, and she wrapped her arms and legs around him. She was so fucking wet that he almost went off just getting them to the bed. "Goddamn, you're beautiful."

"Goddamn, you're fucking hot."

He could hear the smile in her voice as she licked his neck and bit his earlobe. He'd always liked that she talked dirty in bed. "Such language."

"I learned everything from you." Her voice was low and sultry. "Remember?"

And he did. He was her first, and he'd been so horny for her that he'd had to stop a couple of times just to make sure she had the best first experience a man could give. He didn't have to be so patient this time, thank God. She was wet, willing, and about to get all she could handle.

Dumping her in the middle of the bed got her laugh—and he got an eyeful as her gorgeous breasts bounced and her legs spread to help keep her steady. "Spread your legs wider for me," he demanded.

Shelby sucked in a breath, all laughter gone as she obeyed his command. Her glittering gaze was on him as he reached toward his drawer and retrieved a handful of condoms. Once would not be enough. One night might never be enough.

"You don't have to use those," she said, her voice catching. "I've been on the pill for years. I want to *feel* every bare inch of you."

"Jesus, Shel. You're killing me." But he threw the condoms back into the drawer.

She held out her arms. "I want you to love me."

SHELBY MEANT MORE than with his body, but he didn't have to know that yet. He was finally naked and willing, instead of hiding. And dear God, he turned her on. She lay there completely open as he looked at her. Like some Viking raider eyeing his prize.

"Touch yourself," he commanded.

"You too," she replied, as her hands roamed her breasts. She kneaded the round globes and plucked at her hard nipples, the anticipation of the moment making every sensation spike. Leaving one hand on her breasts, she snaked the other down her belly toward the source of some sweet agony. Shelby was so hot she couldn't even tease herself, instead she plunged two fingers inside to fill the emptiness.

"Fuck," he groaned as he stroked his shaft. "Take your fingers out of there, that's mine."

And then he was on her, his weight pressing her down into the soft mattress as he took her mouth. His teeth scraped against hers in a battle of tongues and lips. Lacing their fingers, he moved her hands above her head. He kissed and nipped the corners of her mouth before moving down the side of her neck. Then he bit the skin that joined her neck and shoulder, she almost came.

He remembered. She cried out, because that spot was a major erotic zone. Goose bumps broke out all over her body, and her back arched. God, she missed this—she missed him. No one had ever made her feel like a pure sexual being the way he did. He blasted through barriers to bombard her senses and overwhelm her. And she loved it. This was the most basic feeling, the primitive side that needed to mate. "I want you inside me," she said. "Now."

"No." He continued assaulting her body with kisses. Using one hand to keep hers above her head, he shifted slightly to uncover her body. But his thighs kept her pinned and unable to move. She writhed and thrashed as he played her body, and she couldn't do anything but take his attention.

Mike's free hand shaped and molded her breasts, squeezing and plumping them so her nipples were rock hard and aching. Only then did he use his mouth. Sucking and licking, he drove her into a frenzy.

Her hips bucked, and she tossed her head back and forth, moaning. He covered her mouth with his in a long drugging kiss. "Shhh, we don't want to wake up anyone."

"I don't think I care," she said, breathlessly.

His grin sparked her own and then he was back to her breasts. "Damn shame you have to put these into a bra."

Shelby sighed as he kissed the undersides of each breast and then moved lower. "Don't I know it."

Her belly contracted as Mike's mouth travelled over the slightly rounded curve there. He didn't linger, but moved lower to the heat of her. "Hmmm, shaved."

Yesss. His mouth was on her. One long lick, and she came unglued. Shuddering and shaking, she was so fucking close. But she wanted him inside of her when she came. When she realized that her eyes were squeezed shut, she opened them wide. No way was she missing the erotic sight of this strong, sexy man feasting on her body.

Belatedly, Shelby realized her hands were free, and she reached down to run her fingers into his hair. He lapped at her opening and sucked on her hidden bundle of nerves, making her arousal shoot up into the stratosphere. How was it possible to sustain it and survive? "Mike, I need you to fuck me, now."

He chuckled. "Yes, ma'am."

But he took his time, stroking her legs and kissing the insides of her thighs. He stopped at her ankles and bit the arch of her foot. The nip surprised a giggle out of her and then a sigh as he kissed her and moved slowly back the way he'd come. Climbing up her body, he rubbed himself over her skin, until they were chest to breast. The skin-to-skin contact showcased the differences in their bodies. Hers soft and his hard.

His lips teased her and she opened on a sigh, just as he stroked into her wet depths. One long slide that stretched her in a way that she hadn't felt in more than fifteen years. He was a big man, but she was more than ready for the invasion. She welcomed it. She needed it. "Yesss," she moaned.

"You're so tight."

She thought it was praise but couldn't say anything in return. Because he was moving, rocking in and out of her in a rhythm that had her digging her nails into his back. Her knees were bent as Shelby met him thrust for thrust. He was taking her his way, ignoring her impatience. "You feel so good. Why did you have to wait so long?" she moaned.

But he didn't answer, just kissed her as he picked up the pace. This was no gentle reconnection, this was pure animal lust and she loved every inch. Mike took her the way she'd been dreaming about. Slow and then harder. Slamming in and out of her as their passion rose.

His muscles bunched in his arms as he adjusted his position. "Hold on," he told her, his face a mask of passion. Sitting back on his heels, he had her legs over his forearms as he angled their bodies. After pulling out all the way, he pushed back inside and the penetration was so deep that her inner muscles started contracting. Her whole body was going to ignite in an explosion of pleasure. "Oh God, yes. Mike. Oh."

She threw back her head, no longer watching him, only taking what he gave her. In and out, hard and fast, he rocked the bed and her world. And she held onto him, because he was her anchor in this sea of carnality. The expression on his face was pure decadence, as if she were the finest wine he'd ever tasted and it drove her pleasure higher. "Mike!"

"Come for me, Shel," he gritted out.

And then she did. The orgasm ripped through her so powerfully she saw stars and fireworks and every other thing that she wrote about in her songs that had never happened with anyone else but him. No other man had ever done what this man did to her body. To her heart.

To her soul.

A second later, he came, hoarsely shouting her name as he spilled himself inside of her.

His head was thrown back in ecstasy, and he was everything to her. All male. Strong but caring and so passionate that it made her thighs quiver. Letting down her legs, he lay on top of her, holding his full weight off her with his elbows as he kissed her.

Still inside her body, he touched her with a tenderness that made her heart swell with love. A love that he wouldn't believe because he thought she would walk away again. Shelby had seen that in his eyes when he looked at her.

She thought tonight was a victory of sorts. He finally

gave in and made love to her. And oh Lordy was it something. A jackhammer was needed to get the smile off her face.

"Wow," she said. That was as eloquent as she could manage in her post multiple-climax glow.

"We're still pretty good together, huh?"

Her eyebrows shot up into her hairline. "Pretty good? That was incredible." She kissed his nose and scraped her nails in his hair before tugging it just hard enough to bring his lips to hers. "You're still the master."

"And you'll get more than you can handle if you keep kissing me like that."

Shelby grinned and contracted her inner muscles, squeezing him gently. "What do you mean?" she asked, interjecting as much innocence into her voice as she could manage without laughing.

He growled at her and it started all over again. The magic, the wonder, the pleasure that was almost too much to bear. But she did, and she didn't even care that she might not walk the next day.

Mike was hers, and he was everything she'd been dreaming of.

DANI DUPREE LOOKED at her husband over the file she'd been reading. "This will be a problem."

"This whole mess is a problem. How the hell was all this missed?" Damon said.

They were in a plush hotel room in the heart of Nashville, both sitting on the king-size bed with a stack of files laid out around them. "Look what we had to go through to get all this. But we were looking for something that wasn't quite right. Overworked detectives with enormous caseloads wouldn't make these connections. And certainly not over multiple jurisdictions."

Damon smiled at her. "Always the champion for the underdog."

"Hey, with all the targets painted on officers' backs lately, they need a break every now and then."

He held up a hand. "I'm on your side."

Dani smiled back. "I know. I'm just glad we're getting all this together. Thank God, for all those military contacts you have."

"What do I always say?"

"Once a Marine, always a Marine." She answered immediately and with pride.

"Damn skippy."

"Should we call Mike?"

Damon shook his head. "He's headed back to Phoenix with Shelby Lynn and the kid for those rehearsals tomorrow. Might as well let him get some sleep. I want to make contact with that retired case worker in the morning to see what she has to say. We'll call Mike as soon as we can give him everything."

"I married such a smart man," she teased.

"Smart enough to marry a doctor."

Dani reached over and ran a finger down his naked chest. "We should probably get some sleep too." She made her tone as sultry as she could manage.

Damon immediately started moving files off the bed, dropping them into a pile on the floor. "Yes, we should."

The fact that the hour was well after midnight before they were sated enough to sleep didn't bother Dani in the least. She couldn't be happier. She patted her still-flat tummy in the dark while listening to her husband's deep, even breathing. The little secret she was keeping could wait a little longer.

After this concert, she would break the news to her husband and their friends. She was officially done traveling overseas with the CDC. Dani was staying home to open a practice of her own because in about seven months, she was going to have another Dupree in her life.

Or maybe two.

Twins did run in the family.

CHAPTER 14

ike had the girls up and moving at dawn, which meant they hit Phoenix at the height of rush-hour traffic. Today was Thursday. Shelby was due at the arena mid-afternoon and would be there until late in the evening for rehearsal and sound checks. The concerts were completely sold out for the weekend.

The truck rolled through the gate at the mansion on Camelback, the girls lying down in the back like before.

Madge waited on the front steps. As soon as the truck stopped, Rebecca was out and running toward the older woman, who stooped down and swept up the little girl into her arms.

"I missed you," Madge said. "And what has you smiling so much?"

"I got to ride a horse," Rebecca said.

Madge almost dropped her, looking at Mike in astonishment.

Mike grinned and shrugged.

To her credit, Madge never let the sudden flow of words faze her after the initial shock. She smiled and ruffled all that blond hair. "I bet that was fun. Are you hungry?"

"Sure," Rebecca said.

"Cook has some chocolate chip pancakes with whipped cream ready for you."

Rebecca waved and took off into the house.

Madge turned back with an eyebrow raised. Then she looked Shelby up and down, and the other eyebrow flew up as well. She turned a very perceptive gaze back to Mike as he unloaded the two bags from the truck. "You've been busy."

"Protect and serve, ma'am." And he wasn't saying a damn thing about the curious look she was shooting them. She could speculate all she wanted. to the decision was Shelby's if she wanted to say anything about the fantastic night she'd just spent in his bed.

And their lovemaking didn't change anything.

Shelby was a famous singer and, while she said she was retiring, she was just too young to give all that up. Performing was in her blood. The same way being a detective was in his.

Once the bags were inside, he turned to go. Time for him to get back to finding this killer. Nodding to Madge, he grabbed Shelby by the hand and walked with her back outside. "Extra police officers will be assigned to the arena while you're rehearsing today. Stay within sight of either them or your personal security team the whole time."

"I will," she said.

Mike frowned down into her earnest face. "I mean it. I don't care if you have to bring someone into the bathroom with you—you're not alone for one moment."

"I'm sure it'll be fine. You worry too much."

"And you don't worry enough."

She reached up and cupped the side of his face, her smooth fingers rubbing the stubble there.

He loved the feel of her hands on him.

"Will I see you tonight?"

Mike nodded. If he didn't need to be at work, he wouldn't be leaving now, but his people had been busy over his days off, and he wanted to look at the case. But he'd be with her every night until this was over. For however long it lasted, she was his to protect. "I'll be here." Her smile made his heart catch.

"I love sleepovers."

"This doesn't involve manicures or itching powder in my shorts, does it?"

"Only if you fall asleep before I do."

He leaned down and kissed her, long and hard. "I better make sure I wear you out then."

Her breath caught and she went all liquid in his arms, and he had to fight the urge to take her into the house and start wearing her out now. But they both had business to attend, even if his body wasn't happy with moving away from her tempting self. "See that you do."

Shelby turned away as he got into his truck. He loved to watch that woman walk—either toward him or away, the view was spectacular. She turned and blew him a kiss. She used to do that in the old days, and it made his heart ache. When this ended . . .

He didn't want to think about that yet. Better to focus on the case.

Just then his cell rang.

CROUCHING BEHIND THE A/C unit on the roof of the huge house next door, he was frozen with rage. His earlier happiness with finding a camouflaged vantage point that let him see the courtyard and pool of Shelby's house faded.

She hadn't even been home.

All this time, she hadn't even been fucking home. She'd been off with that man. Kissing him and probably more. Who the hell was he?

Whore, just like all the others. Spreading their legs for any dick. The voice slithered through him, and this time he let it. Because the shadow was always right.

And you thought she was special, the voice mocked.

He felt the hot shame wash over him at the derisive tone. He had thought she was different, with her soft voice and pretty songs. She'd seen all his work, and she hadn't understood.

And maybe that was it. She just didn't understand they were meant for each other.

She doesn't want you, maggot. And she never will.

He gave himself a half-hearted slap to the side of his head. He was trying so hard not to listen, but the voice inside him was so strong. Too powerful to resist anymore. "She just needs to understand. Tomorrow," he whined. "When we're together, I'll make her see she means everything to me."

And the shadow laughed.

After he had Shelby, he would demand the name of the man she'd been with. No other man had the right to come between Shelby and him. Only one other man had even tried, and he'd made sure to erase that threat.

He'd erase this one as well.

~

"Wolfe."

"The big, bad?"

"That one's been done before," he muttered. Hearing Casey's amused laugh made Daniel smile. He was waiting for Mike to get to the office so they could go over everything

139

new in the case. Since he was basically twiddling his thumbs, her call was a welcome distraction.

"I'll work harder next time, but I've been up most of the night putting together the file on vic number two."

"Did you find out who she was?" Not that a name helped find the missing woman, but any information was good in a case like this.

"Yes, and at great personal danger to myself, I might add."

"How's that?"

"Have you ever had to deal with grumpy dentists? Well, let me tell you, they're not a fun lot. This one better be glad he's a state away, because I have half a mind to drive over to New Mexico and kick his ass."

Daniel sat forward in his chair. New Mexico? So maybe their theory about the killer was correct. "She's actually *from* New Mexico?"

"Born and raised. Name is Amy Young, and she liked her meth, which is why I was up to my ass in grumpy dentists. She had a couple of crowns with designs on them."

"I didn't even know that was a thing."

Casey snorted. "Welcome to the twenty-first century. It's basically a tooth tattoo, and only a handful of places will even do designs on crowns. This girl clearly had folks with money, because these things aren't cheap."

"One more clue to this whole thing. Thanks, Casey."

"Is Mike back yet?"

"He's due in any minute."

"Good. I'm sending you an email with the info and the name of the detective in Las Cruces who is anxiously awaiting contact for this girl. This is his missing person's case."

"You normally go above and beyond on this kind of thing?" Daniel was curious because making contact with another jurisdiction wasn't the norm. Doing so wasn't part of her job description, but the medical examiners he'd heard about weren't usually willing to go beyond the dead body and crime scene details.

"This guy is pissing me off. Besides, I owe Mike a couple of favors. A little extra leg work for him is a small return on a big debt. But now I'm headed home to get sleep and maybe a slice of cold pizza."

"I'll let Mike know as soon as I see him. Enjoy the cold pizza."

"Yep." And then she was gone.

Mike was one of those guys. He inspired the people around him. The fact he'd done a couple of big favors for a friend made him exceptional. Daniel was proud to be working in a department under him. He was learning so much, mostly by example. And he had his own news. He'd tracked down those damn rodents. The information had come in about ten minutes prior to Casey's call. Daniel wanted to run it by Mike before he called over to Nashville PD and had them check it out.

This was the piece of evidence that could tie the killer to the scene of at least one of the murders. The only clue they had, and it would be important, he could just feel it.

His cell chirped, and the number belonged to dispatch. "Wolfe," he said.

"This is Kris in dispatch, we have a homicide," she said. "The street sergeant asked for Mike specifically, but I have you listed as the callout detective until noon."

He dropped his head on the desk. They didn't have time for another homicide, but if patrol asked for Mike, then maybe it was connected. He'd keep his fingers crossed. The dispatch supervisor was thorough as she gave him the details she had. "What's the address?"

She rattled it off. Another warehouse in central Phoenix.

"I'm on my way, and I'll call Mike."

"Thanks," she said, and the relief in her voice was clear. "The sergeant said it's really bad, just so you know."

"Copy that."

Daniel had a sick feeling that this was their missing woman, Tara. The call was sooner than they expected, and everyone had been holding out some kind of hope that she'd be found alive. It was a false hope, but they'd all had it. Even while systematically checking the hundreds of abandoned warehouses that littered Phoenix.

"Damn." He grabbed his notebook, a pen, and checked his phone. He'd call Mike from the car and hopefully catch him driving, that way they could just meet up at the scene. He dialed the number he didn't realize he'd memorized.

"Just couldn't stay away, huh?" Casey said. But her tone was grim.

"You heard?"

"Just now. Looks like I'm booking in more OT, because there's no way in hell you and Mike are going to this scene without me."

"I thought you might feel that way. You have the address?"

"Yes. And if I get you off my phone, I'll be out there with a tech before you've even had the chance to miss the sound of my voice."

"Fine." He hung up—a little game they seemed to be playing. Who got the last word.

He was in the car when he called Mike, only to find out Mike was almost there already. That man was seriously plugged in to the street units. Someone must have called him directly, and now Daniel had to haul ass to catch up.

Again.

The drive took about ten minutes to get there, but when he did, he was happy to see he'd at least beaten Casey. Mike's truck was parked off to the side, as were half a dozen police cars. Crime scene tape was already up, and the morose expressions of the officers let him know more than anything that this would be worse than anything he'd seen yet. Cops had the ability to maintain a sense of humor over most everything. They all called it 'gallows humor," but the levity was noticeably absent.

One younger officer sat half in and half out of his patrol car with his head in his hands. His partner talked to him, squatted down with a reassuring hand on the young man's shoulder.

Daniel passed them on his way and the haunted look both their eyes made him pause. "Just how bad is it?" he asked.

They both looked up and shook their heads. "Worst I've ever seen," the older one said.

What the hell happened between the last murder and this one to make the scene so much worse? Curious about the minds of psychopaths, Daniel had been reading journals on the subject in his spare time. There must have been some kind of new trigger.

Mike stepped out of the warehouse as Daniel approached the door. He stopped dead in his tracks at the expression on his boss's face. He'd never seen such a look before. Even the rage he'd glimpsed at the last scene hadn't been as feral, as determined, or as sickened as the one on Mike's face in that moment. "What the hell happened?"

Mike took a deep breath. "He realized Shelby was gone."

Daniel frowned. "How could he know that? You were careful to get them both out of the house without anyone seeing anything."

"He must have been watching somehow. It's the only thing that makes sense, considering the carnage inside. I'd be willing to guess Casey will put the time of death sometime after we left for Flagstaff."

Daniel didn't question the hypothesis. Mike was eerily accurate about these things. "Is it like one of her videos?"

"No." Then the big man let out a breath. "This is a very different scene from the previous two. This one is the sickest fucker I've ever seen."

"Jesus," Daniel muttered. Now he really didn't want to go inside. But viewing evidence was part of his job and if he advanced the way he wanted to, then he'd be the homicide sergeant one day. He couldn't let a scene destroy him. "I'll take a quick look, and then come back out and wait for the medical examiner."

Mike nodded and turned his body slightly to the side, giving his tacit permission.

As Daniel moved to pass, he was stopped by Mike's hand.

"Don't step too far into the room, the blood is everywhere."

Daniel nodded. "Got it. Anything else?"

"The shock value is high. Try and keep it together when you come back outside." Mike nodded toward the cops all watching them from a distance. "They need to know we'll take care of this."

Taking a deep breath of the fresh air, Daniel said, "I won't let you down."

"I know."

Mike moved around him and headed toward the young officer still sitting in the patrol car.

Daniel figured he must have been the first unit on scene, since he looked worse than anyone else. Peer support would get called out, and they'd all be in for a de-brief once the scene was thoroughly secured and the officers released.

As with the other scenes, the smell is what hit him first. Maybe he was psyching himself out due to what Mike said, but the odor of death seemed so much stronger. And when he stepped inside the main portion of the warehouse, he could see why. He almost went to his knees.

Instead, he braced a hand on the door and closed his eyes.

Sick bastard. He took a moment before he could talk himself into opening them again. Carnage wasn't even the right word to describe the scene because what had been done to that poor woman was nothing less than butchery. "Dear God," he whispered.

She was in pieces. Everywhere.

This was no body dump and stage set. The murder had happened right there in the center of the room. Blood spatter lined the walls and the floor, and body parts were flung in every direction, as if dismembering her hadn't been enough.

Daniel forced himself to stand there and take it all in. The violence—the terror that stained the air. The abject horror of mangled flesh and entrails twisted in a mass that didn't resemble anything human. And when he was sure his expression was under control, he walked outside.

But the world didn't look the same as when he went inside. The vicious murders of the first two women hadn't affected him the way this one did. Mike had been right. They had to keep it together for their brothers in blue, because *this* was their job. To find and capture the animal that went beyond the normal scope of reasoning.

Casey and her tech arrived at that moment and not even her newly spiked red hair could bring a smile to Daniel's face. He stayed to the side as Mike talked to her. Her mobile face was set in a grimace.

She nodded once and then followed Mike toward the door of the warehouse. The tech stayed behind gathering supplies. Casey had only her camera in her hands. She was fastidious about making sure the crime scene was carefully preserved in photos before they started mucking around gathering evidence, as she called it.

He didn't go with them. Not yet. And he'd made the right decision. The subtle shake of Mike's head as he passed told Daniel to stay where he was for the moment. The instant relief he felt was both appalling and necessary. He needed a couple of minutes to make sure he didn't throw up. The bile was at the back of his throat, and he held it at bay by sheer strength of will.

He'd never felt like taking justice in his own hands before. Daniel was all about the legal system and making it work, but in this moment, he had the grisly realization he could kill another man in cold blood. The animal doing this didn't deserve to rot away in a cage.

This monster needed to die.

CHAPTER 15

"They're calling him "The Surgeon" in the newspaper," Madge said.

The disgust in her voice was thick. Shelby looked up from the schedule she'd been making changes to. "Who makes up these things?"

"I guess they can't call every killer "The Sadistic Butcher." That wouldn't sell any papers, or have folks tuned into the news stations. Every new one gets a catchy name."

Shaking her head, Shelby glanced across the stage to check on Rebecca. But the little girl was surrounded by her dolls and a couple of new toy horses. She'd retreated back into her quiet self, but the silence wasn't like before. She was still talking, thank God. Even if all she talked about were horses and when she'd get to ride Cinnamon again.

"That murder is a form of entertainment for the news people is just sick."

"I'm sure they're all high-fiving when a poor person gets mutilated, because then their ratings all go up."

"When are we done here?" Shelby asked, ready to change the subject. She was tired and had worked hard with her band and the sound technicians most of the morning. Her hairdresser/make-up artist was a pro and didn't need anything more than approval on a new lipstick color she wanted to use for the Friday performance. The wardrobe was ready and waiting, having already been fitted before she left with Mike during the week.

"I have to check a couple more items off my list, but I think we're good to go." Madge had her clipboard out and was making notes here and there in the ten pages located there.

"Good. It's getting late, and I want to get Rebecca home and serve her a hot meal."

"Will the hot detective be there?"

Shelby shot a look around, but no one was close within ear shot. A couple of the sound guys were in deep conversation with her guitarist, and someone with the lighting crew was setting up a ladder on the stage at the other end. "Don't say that too loudly," she whispered.

"I didn't, but your reaction is interesting. I'll go ahead and call the Chef and let her know to set another place at the table."

Shelby felt her ears get hot. Madge wouldn't judge if she decided to come out on stage stark naked in front of a hundred thousand fans, but having her know Mike would be spending the night felt naughty somehow. Especially since Madge was more like her mother than just her manager. And who knew when Mike would even be there? He was back and focused on the job.

"I guess." Shelby stood to go get Rebecca. Madge's amused chuckle followed her.

She reached the little girl, and Rebecca looked up and smiled. "Time to go?"

Shelby nodded. "Did you have fun today?"

Rebecca shrugged and started putting away her toys in the bag she had.

A gray-and-white sock monkey caught Shelby's attention. "Where did that come from?" She didn't remember that particular toy.

Rebecca shrugged again.

Chills ran the length of Shelby's body. There was no reason to be worried about a stupid toy, but for some reason it bothered her. "When did you find it exactly?" She tried to keep her voice neutral.

"After lunch." Rebecca stood and slung the strap of the bag across her little body. "Okay, ready."

Shelby couldn't stop from glancing around or the feeling of being watched, but she ignored it. Being back in town was making her jumpy, but the security team hadn't left her side all day. She didn't want to cause a scene over a toy, especially since they were about to leave, but the stuffed animal gave her a bad feeling. She'd ask Madge about it when they were home.

Two men who were part of the security team approached her on the stage. "Ready to go, ma'am?"

"Yes, thank you for being here with us."

"Our pleasure," the older one said.

His name was Hank, and he was the leader of her security team. Shelby liked all the guys, and they never let on that this was a pain for them in any way. Of course, Madge was paying them quite a bit of money not to mind, but they seemed genuine enough.

"We're leaving a car and a team member here for Ms. Henner, but I know you're ready to go. Shall we?"

Good ol'Madge. She never missed a beat. The feeling of being watched slowly faded as they left the arena, and Shelby shook it off as an over-tired imagination. All of their people were checked, and double checked. She had nothing to worry about as long as she stayed with her team. And she had no plans to do otherwise. She might be stubborn about doing these shows, but she wasn't stupid. She was happy to have extra security. These concerts would be the best of her career. Her fans deserved the best that she had to give, especially since they were her last.

∼

MIKE WAS STILL at the scene as dusk darkened into night. The remains of Tara Shumway had been removed, and they had a positive ID this time, due to Tara's love of butterfly tattoos. She had several on her body, and all had been found and confirmed.

Casey had packed up and her tech was more than ready to go. He'd been chain smoking by their van for an hour now, waiting on her to finish up.

Mike thought he'd quit about six months ago, but Casey said this case was stressing out the poor guy and he'd picked up the habit again. She had a betting pool going at work on how long he'd make it before he quit the job completely. Casey didn't think he'd last a full year—he was at eight months now. Looking at him while he paced, Mike thought she might be right. That kid wasn't cut out for this type of work.

"I've got everything," Casey said, coming up behind him.

"Thanks. Call me if you need anything."

She put a hand on his arm and squeezed. "You'll get this guy."

He looked down into her earnest face. The spikey red hair made her look like a rebellious teenager, especially since she wasn't wearing any make-up. "Go home and sleep. Your eyes are the color of your hair."

"Gee, Mike. Is that your way of saying I look like shit?"

"Yeah, it is. Go home. You can let someone else process everything tomorrow."

"Are you going home?"

They both knew he wasn't. But not for the reasons she thought. "I'll get there . . . eventually."

"Me too." Then she nodded at Detective Wolfe and left.

"What's our move, boss?" Daniel said, coming up next to him.

"Have the patrol sergeant start sending his guys home, as soon as a couple more swing shift officers arrive. I want this scene locked up tight in case this bastard comes back to visit."

"You think he will?"

Mike looked around at the shadows lengthening between the buildings. Traffic horns intermittently blared on the freeway that curved away and to the south of their location. The air smelled like old diesel and rubber, due to the tire recycling plant a block away. It was a desolate place to die. Surrounded by more than a million people, and yet utterly alone in an abandoned warehouse-turned slaughter house. "No, I don't. I think if he was inclined to visit one of his scenes, it wouldn't be this one."

"Because this one's different?"

"This was about rage and hate. Nothing was staged about this scene. Nothing—beautiful—to him."

Daniel's face let Mike know he didn't like the description, and he didn't either. But this killer had taken so much time with the other two women, posing them in such a way, as well as tailor designing his own videos that he must consider himself a bit of an artist. To him, the carved-up women and the scenes he staged were his art.

What he considered the mess he'd left here, Mike didn't know, but he hoped to God that Shelby didn't get an email of this scene. She already had nightmares as it was, something he'd learned while they were away. "Let's get out of here. You brought the case file with you?"

Daniel nodded. "I wanted to go over it with you in person."

"Good. Follow me. I have a meeting to attend, and you might as well come along."

The drive lasted longer than he was interested in, considering how tired he suddenly was, but the food and company were well worth it. From the truck, he'd called Shelby to make sure they'd made it home safely. The units stationed around her home for extra patrol had already reported in, but he'd wanted to hear her voice.

"I was hoping you'd make it here for dinner," she said.

"I have some things to do before I can make it."

"What happened? I can hear in your voice that something's gone wrong."

"I'll tell you about it when I get there."

"Okay, just be careful. I'll be waiting up."

"You should sleep, I can crash on one of the couches in the den."

"Not if I have anything to say about it, Mike Hanson. You're so goddamn stubborn."

The steel in her voice made him smile. She was so feisty when she was riled. "Yes, ma'am."

"I'll see you soon." Then she hung up.

He let her have her way. And she thought *he* was the stubborn one. That woman put mules to shame.

The lights blazed from the house where he parked. A rental, the house was one of the many his friends used when they all came into Phoenix. It wasn't quite as large as the one Shelby was staying in, but it was big enough to house three families easily. Which it was at the moment.

Daniel pulled in and joined him at the curb. "Just what kind of meeting are we having?"

"Counsel of war is more apt, but the food will be great."

The door opened, and a large shadow filled the entrance.

Mike almost started laughing when Daniel uttered a string of curse words under his breath. "Don't worry, he's almost over the fact that you had a crush on Elizabeth."

"I don't think he'll ever be over that," Daniel muttered. "If this comes to blows, I'm blaming you for bringing me here."

"Come on, Wolfe. Don't tell me you're worried."

"About another pissed-off Marine, especially one that's bigger than I am? Hell yeah."

"I won't let him hurt you." Mike laughed.

Zach's frown was ferocious but Mike thought he saw a little bit of humor there as well. "You know Elizabeth will be pissed if you hit him," he said as he passed the big man.

Zach nodded once and turned back into the house, without saying anything to Daniel.

Mike ushered him inside. "That went better than I expected."

"If you say so."

"Just don't make eye contact with her."

"How am I supposed to do that?"

The frustration was there in the plaintive question. Mike couldn't help it, he burst out laughing and patted Daniel on the back. "God only knows."

The main room was filled with adults and kids running around. Damon and Dani were getting hugs from the kids, while Lily and Elizabeth handed out drinks. Zach hovered over his wife, and Jesse laughed over something Damon said. The atmosphere was happy chaos and Mike could feel his shoulders begin to relax. He'd been tense all day, but Shelby was safe at home and all his friends were in one place.

"Daniel," Elizabeth exclaimed in delight. "I didn't know you were coming." She smiled and started toward him, only to stop, turn, and go back toward her husband. Planting a hand on one hip and using the other to beckon her husband's head down to hers, she whispered in his ear.

Mike was amused to see that everyone in the room had gotten quiet just in time to hear her say that he'd better not hit the man who'd been heroic enough to take a bullet for her.

"And I love *you*," she finished off her speech with a nod.

Daniel's face was priceless and a little red around the ears. And then everyone started laughing and talking at once. A few moments and a couple of introductions later, they all settled down to have burgers and hotdogs, and no one ended up in a fight.

Mike separated his friends from their wives after dinner, and they headed out to the casita in the backyard.

The men were all business as soon as the door closed. Even Zach.

"Thank you all for being here," Mike said.

"Hey," Damon said, "we all owe you one. This is what we're here for."

"Just tell us what you need," Jesse said.

Mike looked around at his friends. The best group of guys he'd ever known. He was damned lucky to have these men on his side. And now that they were all together, he felt more confident that he could protect Shelby and Rebecca. Five ex-Marines against one psychopath.

That asshole didn't have a chance.

CHAPTER 16

"So you think Rebecca's father was this Charles Weston?" Mike asked.

He looked around the table at his friends. They had schematics of the arena, a plan for Shelby's protection, and even an escape route if necessary. Nothing was left to chance. The wives and kids had been upgraded to the VIP section for the Sunday night show, per Shelby and Madge, so they would be in one place for safety.

And having Zach standing guard meant no one was getting through. Period.

With security settled, they'd turned to the mystery surrounding Rebecca's father and how this killer was connected. Because it was becoming clear that somehow, this was all part of the same big picture.

Damon nodded and pulled out a piece of paper. "And if Shelby wants to be sure, we can match up Rebecca's DNA to his because it's on file now."

Daniel pulled out the folder with his notes and a couple of faxes in it. "That's the name I came up with while I was hunting down that chinchilla hair. Not much call for chinchilla pets in Nashville so the store owner still had receipts for his sales going back a couple of years. Charles Weston has a matched set, and he was fanatical about their food and cages. I wanted to run the details by you before having Nashville PD check it out, but if he's dead, then I'm out of ideas."

"So who has the chinchillas now?" Jesse asked.

"And who's Nashville's suspect in that homicide?" Mike asked.

"I think it's the same person," Damon said. "And I think he's your killer here in Phoenix."

"This sounds like the opening of one of Beth's books. We need beer. Who wants one?" Zach asked. He returned with five long-necks and passed them around. "Okay, continue."

Damon mock-saluted with his beer. "Charles Weston was a semi-talented musician with a drinking problem. He'd been fired from almost every job he had due to his alcoholism and history of violence. But, he was good looking and a ladies' man, according to the folks we tracked down. With a little charm, he talked himself into every job easily. Especially, when a woman was in charge of the hiring."

"So, he was on tour with Shelby's opening act for about a year?" Mike asked. That must have been how he'd made contact with Abby. "Who hired him?"

"The stage manager at the time was a woman." Damon looked through his papers and nodded. "But Madge had him fired for his constant absences and the other stage manager as well, because he wasn't her first bad hire." He flipped the page and looked over more of his notes. "He worked locally as a lighting technician when no one would hire him as a musician any longer."

"So who killed Abby? Charles or the man who killed him?" Zach wondered.

"No way to know, but either Charles did in one of his

violent moments or the new guy did, maybe because of Charles," Mike said.

Jesse sighed. "Without her body, nothing can be proved anyhow. The theories are all supposition on our part."

"The question is, who did Charles trust enough to let into his home for a good length of time?" Daniel asked. He'd been quietly reading the reports from the homicide scene. "Because the boxes of food and trash all around were there before the murder, not after like they originally thought. So his killer was living with him."

Damon beamed at the man before he looked over at Mike. "I like him, he's quick. Glad you're on board with us," he said to Daniel.

And if Zach rolled his eyes, no one said anything, but Mike grinned.

"That was my question as well," Damon said. "So we started looking into his family and came up with very little. His parents are dead, but an estranged aunt had a son about ten years younger than Charles. Weird thing was that, we couldn't find any information on the cousin. It's like he'd just fallen off the face of the planet, until we started looking out of state."

"His name is Larry Ashbrooke, and he's been in and out of psych hospitals his entire life for schizophrenia with violent tendencies. His fingerprints were at the apartment, and he has a record with the state, so the police made the match. They have him down as a person of interest, but there's no evidence he killed Charles, only that he was in the apartment. And since he hasn't been located, he's a dead end."

"Damn," Mike said. "That fits though. Two crime scenes were calm and calculated, but the last one was a nightmare, completely disorganized. A schizophrenic couldn't control himself all the time, especially if he gets mad."

"We found a retired case worker who opened up, doctor

to doctor, with Dani. This kid was a mess and had some kind of hero worship of his cousin, Charles. Apparently, Larry spent summers with Charles and his parents up until the age of thirteen. At which point, something happened to send Larry into a psych hospital until he was eighteen and legally could check himself out, pending doctor approval."

"Jesus Christ," Jesse said. "Some doctor let that messed-up kid out into the world after being locked up for five years?"

"And how long ago was that?" Daniel asked.

But Mike had a feeling he already knew. It all made sense in some weird way. The hero worship, the mental instability, the violence. This was the guy.

Damon looked up from what he was reading. "Three months before Abby disappeared and Charles was killed."

"I don't suppose you have a current picture?" Zach asked. He'd been fairly quiet through the whole recitation.

"Wouldn't that be easy? But no, not a single one," Damon confirmed. "If his mother had anything, then it was lost long ago. She died when her house caught fire about a year after she had Larry committed. She was into mixing alcohol with her pain pills, so when she passed out with a lit cigarette, the whole house went up. And Charles didn't have anything remotely sentimental. Not even pictures of his own parents."

Mike finished his beer and started to pace. "So Charles was obsessed with Shelby Lynn for either a conquest or whatever, but he never acted on what he felt and instead dated Abby. Maybe he talked to his cousin about his obsession and his affair with Shelby's best friend. Maybe he talked about it so much the obsession became Larry's as well."

Jesse picked up where he left off. "So if Shelby becomes Larry's obsession, then Charles is now a rival because he talks incessantly about it. Probably even more when he's drunk. So Larry kills the rival but takes the cuddly little chinchillas?"

"You want to make sense of crazy guy who just murdered his only living relative?" Zach, as always, cut straight to the heart of the issue. "He probably wasn't allowed any pets in the psych ward. Who knows, maybe they're some kind of present for Shelby."

"We called the hospital where Larry lived," Damon said. "One of those fancy places that look more like a country club than a sanatorium. His mother had plenty of money and as her beneficiary, he had his room paid for until he turned eighteen. At which time he inherited the bulk of the money left over."

"They teach computer hacking at those places?" Daniel asked. "Because that email virus he sent to erase Shelby's email was pretty damned sophisticated for someone in a psych ward most of his teenage years. And how has he stayed so close to her? Is he just following the tour, or is he involved in the process somehow?"

"Well, not hacking, but they do teach computer skills, as well as a host of other things. The place is like a technical school," Damon said. "They prepared him for his adult life and an entry level position for a job. By all accounts, he was a very polite and apt pupil."

"Until he started killing people," Mike said. "We need to find out how he's following her because if he's with the tour somehow, then that's more of a problem than we first thought."

And something they needed to figure out immediately.

The casita-turned-war room was a studio-size apartment and was stocked with chips, beer, and other snacks. Perfect for five guys with a mission. Mike had the background checks on all the employees of Shelby's tour, courtesy of Madge. They divvied them up, and each took a chair to start reading.

The night would be long, but it didn't matter. They were

helping Mike figure this out. And he was confident they would.

Two hours went by before they got something, and Daniel was the one who found it in the last file on his lap. The rest of the guys still had two or three to go. "I think this might be it."

Mike looked up. "Whatcha got?"

"Guy by the name of Robert Charleston, goes by Bobby. He was hired on with the road crew one year ago, but that's not what bothers me. His date of birth puts him in his thirties, but he doesn't have any previous job experience. The note on the side of the application says he wasn't qualified for anything more than baggage handling for the crew, but he was an earnest kid who looked like he'd be a hard worker."

"So what's a guy in his thirties doing with no job experience? And how did the age get overlooked? The note makes it sound like he's a kid," Zach asked.

Mike had a laptop at the table where he'd been sitting. "Give me the full name and date of birth."

Daniel rattled it off and then kept reading. "I think we should call Madge and see if she knows this guy or can refer us to whoever the stage manager is."

"In the meantime, keep reading through the rest of the files. I want to make sure everyone else is squeaky clean," Mike said.

While the guys went back to reading, Mike opened up a secure email to a buddy that worked at the Pentagon. They'd been friends for a number of years, and Mike had given him some valuable intel a couple of times. Needless to say, when Mike asked for information, it came back quickly. About thirty minutes elapsed and by that time, the files had been read over thoroughly and no one else seemed suspicious. The background checks had been competent, but no check was full proof. Those checks were for criminal activity, current warrants, or time served, transgressions of that nature.

Mike leaned away from the laptop. "I know why this guy had no work experience."

"Why?" Daniel asked when the other guys stayed quiet.

"Because Robert Charleston committed suicide on New Year's Day, 2001. He was a patient in the same hospital where Larry was committed and had no surviving family members."

"What do you want to bet Larry's first computer hack was into the hospital itself?" Damon said. "You tend to start with small places that are familiar, like the high school kid who hacks into the school system to change a grade."

Jesse chimed in, "Only Larry got himself a new I.D. Finding the right candidate with no family, or one that was already deceased, would have been easy. But why? What was the point of changing his name?"

"Because Robert Charleston didn't have a criminal record," Mike answered. "He was just a messed-up kid with a history of depression and anxiety. Too old, but otherwise a good fit. So, Larry takes his identity as soon as he leaves the hospital, presumably to get a job."

"Did the report ever state why his mother had Larry committed in the first place?" The question was from Zach.

"The summer Larry was thirteen, he beat up and tried to rape a girl while he was staying with his cousin Charles."

"The girl pressed charges?" Daniel asked.

Mike shook his head. "His cousin Charles found them in the act and beat the shit out of him. After he got out of the hospital they transferred him to the psych ward. The incident was covered up completely. Money must have been exchanged in order to avoid a police report, but the details were in the admitting paperwork to the hospital. His mother wanted him to get counseling and had to explain why."

"There could have been some resentment toward the

cousin for putting a beating on him. Maybe he held the guy responsible for getting him committed," Jesse said.

"Maybe," Mike allowed, still reading through the report.

"Who was the girl?" Zach wanted to know. "That might be the trigger."

Mike scrolled through the email, speed reading. Not until the end did he find what he'd been looking for. He sat back and shook his head. No wonder this kid was fucked up. "She was Charles' girlfriend."

"What do you want to bet Charles put him up to the whole thing?" Zach said. "If he's already got that kind of history with his cousin, then going after Shelby like this makes a kind of twisted sense. What Charles wants, Larry wants. He's fully under the influence of whatever his delusions are."

"Larry only had one visitor the entire time he was admitted. Anyone want to guess who came and saw him regularly?"

"Charles," Damon said.

Mike's cell phone buzzed, and Madge's number appeared on the screen. He stood and moved away from the table before he answered. He wasn't sure why, but dread was snaking it way around his stomach. "This is Mike," he said.

The room had gone quiet as soon as he'd left the table.

"She's gone," she said, through a gasping cry. "She's gone, Mike."

"Take a deep breath for me. Who's gone?"

He could hear Madge take a deep breath in and breathe out, but she was still shaky when she spoke again. "Shelby."

"Tell me what happened." His voice was calm but his mind raced. Shelby wasn't stupid, she wouldn't have gone off by herself. And she would have never left Rebecca, so the only thing that made sense was that she'd been taken. Even as his heart squeezed in his chest, the blood in his veins froze. He had to keep it together.

"Rebecca snuck into the room like she does, and when she came and got me, she was almost hysterical. Now she won't say anything." There was a long pause and then her voice cracked. "There's blood on the patio."

"How much?"

"Just a little, but I know it's hers—"

She'd stopped talking as the sobs took over. "Madge," Mike said, trying to get her attention again. "Have the guards searched the grounds?"

A hiccup and then, "Yes."

"Did they find anything?"

"Just a rope tied to the bedroom balcony rail. They said he must have lowered her out onto the mountain and carried her to a waiting car."

Her voice was stronger now that he was keeping her occupied with questions. "Okay, have your security team pulled into the house and keep Rebecca close. We don't know if he's planning to come back for her as well."

"Oh God, you think he will?"

Mike ran a hand through his hair. "I don't know. But I want you both surrounded by armed guards until we get Shelby back."

"You will get her back, Mike. You have to."

A boulder was lodged in his throat, but he got the words out that she needed to hear. "I'll get her back."

The guys were all on their feet when he turned to face them. The files were put away, and the messes they made were cleared off.

"He has her?" Damon asked.

Mike nodded. Now that he was off the phone, he was momentarily paralyzed by the overwhelming fear that coursed through him.

Goddamn it! He would personally kick the asses of every member of that security team for letting that madman get his hands on Shelby. But he was really pissed at himself. He should have kept her with him, no matter what. What had he been thinking? He'd been thinking that seven men patrolling the grounds would be plenty.

"Mike."

He heard his name but it sounded far away. But then something very big and very angry was in his face. Zach. "Marine!"

Mike snapped out of the dark place he'd been in, as if there were another choice with Zach yelling at him. He stared at his friend, whose face was set in a scowl only inches from his own. He took a deep breath. "Stop breathing fire all over me."

Zach narrowed his eyes. "Get your head out of your ass then."

When he looked around, he realized he was alone with Zach, who looked like he was ready to lay a beating on someone. Probably him. "Where is everyone?"

"Damon is getting our equipment together, Jesse is informing the wives, and Daniel went to make a phone call to a tech he's been working with, to get us some possible locations. And I'm babysitting your ass until you get your shit together."

"I'm here. My head got dark for a minute, but I'm back."

"I've been there," Zach said, his tone only a little less harsh. "Jesse and Damon get it as well, but you spooked your rookie."

"He's never been in love before," Mike said. A confession and a statement. As much as he'd tried to shield himself from her, he couldn't deny Shelby had swept in and taken his heart again.

"Damn right," Zach growled. "Now let's go get her back."

CHAPTER 17

Shelby's head pounded. Her mouth was dry, and the left side of her face throbbed in time with her heart beat. But what scared her was that she couldn't move. It didn't make any sense. And the panic that surfaced was primal when she realized that nothing moved. Not her legs, not her arms, and not her eye lids.

What the hell?

What had happened? Was she in the hospital? Why couldn't she remember anything? Full-blown alarm set in, causing her heart to race and her breathing to speed up, but try as she might, she couldn't force any part of her body to so much as twitch. That's when panic set in. But she fought it. Shelby wasn't sure what was happening but she could feel the terror clawing at her, as if her body was functioning at the most basic level—danger or no danger?

Her mind screamed danger.

She struggled until she was exhausted, no closer to understanding what was happening than when she woke up. Then she thought about Rebecca, and Shelby knew that if she didn't use her brain, she wouldn't figure this out. It took a while and some inner strength she wasn't sure she had but she began to relax. Deep breaths in and out, focusing on slowing her heart rate.

What did she know?

She wasn't home.

And it smelled . . . bad. Like rust and copper—and old garbage. But also dusty, as if she were in an old shed that hadn't been used in some time.

Straining to listen, Shelby heard cars in the distance and the wail of a siren. An old house or abandoned building, maybe.

She was lying on her back. The surface was hard, but without the ability to move her fingers, she couldn't tell what it was. She still had on clothes. Such a minor thing, but the fact was a huge relief in her mind. Not that clothes would stop whatever was about to happen, especially since she couldn't even open her eyes to see.

She was in terrible danger.

And the steadily increasing pain on her left cheek that spread over to her nose reinforced the sudden vision of a fist coming at her face out of the darkness on her patio. She remembered.

Tears welled and spilled through her lids. *Oh God*. She hadn't wanted to believe what all her senses screamed, but it was true. She was in the hands of the maniac. The one so obsessed with her he'd killed other women to remake her videos. What did he have planned for her?

Lost in the desolation of that revelation, she didn't hear the footsteps until they were too close. No time remained to pretend she was still passed out.

"Oh good, you're awake," he said.

The voice was young and hesitant, as if he'd interrupted an afternoon nap. She didn't recognize it. At all.

"I thought you would sleep through everything, Shelby Lynn. And I've been doing so much work for us."

She couldn't have answered if she'd wanted to, but he didn't seem to need anything from her.

"It's early in the morning, you know," he said.

His tone was faintly chiding, as if she'd overslept and made him late.

"Time to get out of those pajamas and into something a little more appropriate. Don't you think? But it's still dark so I can understand why you didn't realize. And I'll have to clean off the blood. It might hurt."

He started humming one of her tunes, and she heard him moving around.

And then he touched her face with a cloth. Dabbing carefully, he moved it over her upper lip and back and forth on the skin between her top lip and her nose.

That must have been the smell of copper and rust. Her own blood. The cloth disappeared, only for her to feel a light sweep of his fingers across her cheek, over her nose and down the side that was bruised. He touched her lips and tickled her earlobes, touching in the way of a lover.

Shelby was creeped out down to her very soul. She wanted to throw up and shrink away from the vile touch.

He moved her arms. Once they were above her head, he took the edges of her overlarge t-shirt and began moving it upward and off her body. He touched her here and there, caressing her—and shattering her.

Shelby started screaming. The sound ricocheted around her brain, but the only thing that emerged was a strangled hiss. Then she started praying.

Not for God to help her. No, that wouldn't do at all. Shelby started praying for something better than a miracle.

She prayed for Mike.

Because he would find her. Shelby just had to survive until he did.

~

FIVE WORRIED EX-MARINES showed up at Shelby's mansion, in black fatigues and armed like they were about to invade a small country. Mike led the group.

The first person to approach them was the leader of the security team. His problem was that he got too close.

Mike didn't lose control. But he wanted to.

"You'd better tell this very large, very angry man how Shelby Lynn got abducted during your watch before he hits you," Jesse told the man. They all towered over the guy.

His name was Hank, and he took a quick gulp and a deep breath before he answered. "I would deserve it, but I haven't been sitting around doing nothing since she was taken."

Mike nodded. "Tell me everything."

The guys all gathered around, except for Daniel, who stepped away to make a phone call. He was calling dispatch to coordinate. A missing person's detective was on his way to take a statement from Madge and an "attempt to locate" message had been sent to every patrol car in the Phoenix Metro area. Daniel was doing everything he could to make sure the proper people were involved. They'd all agreed to that.

Mike wasn't waiting for proper channels. Shelby didn't have that kind of time.

"I put Rebecca, and the Chef into the den. Two of my guys and one of yours are in there and will be until this is over." Hank threw a look at Madge, who paced close to Daniel, listening to his side of the phone conversation. "Her we can't control."

"Good," Mike said. Over his shoulder he said, "Zach, take the bedroom. Second floor, third door on the right."

Zach took off at a run. He was the best tracker of the group, so if a trail or clue was left behind, he'd find it. The rest of them looked back at Hank.

"Continue," Mike said.

"This guy had to be watching the house for a while to get the pattern of our patrols. And we varied it, so he must have gotten lucky there. I had your guys going door-to-door, to see if anyone had seen something odd in the area."

"Good move," Mike said, clenching his fists. He spoke barely above a growl, and he still considered hitting the guy, but knew it was really himself that he wanted to hit. He should have been here, damn it.

"The neighbor next door is on vacation according to the maid and she is older, so rarely goes outside. But she swears she thought someone was on the roof a couple of nights ago."

"Jess," Mike said, without breaking eye contact with a visibly nervous Hank.

Jesse nodded. "I'm on it."

"I'm assuming you found something useful, otherwise you wouldn't be wasting my time?" Mike asked.

"Yes, sir. Two houses down, the family has the wife's mother living with them and she walks her little dog all over the neighborhood. She's also the self-appointed block-watch captain so she looks for unusual things. She told us about an older model, tan Toyota Camry that's been in the area lately. She never saw the driver, but she wrote down the license plate so she could call the police if it showed up again. She didn't go out today because the dog was sick, so she's not a witness to anything but the car being there, but she supplied the plate number. She swears that car does not belong to anyone in this neighborhood."

"I think you just saved the rest of your teeth," Damon

said. "I'll take that." Once he had the paper with the plate info, he pulled out his cell phone to make a call.

Mike turned away to check on the progress of Daniel's conversation. He hoped Hank took the hint and went back inside, because he was holding his temper by both hands, and control was slipping.

"Missing persons did a call out and have as many bodies on the street as they can," Daniel said.

"What about Lance? You said he was working on finding a pattern for this guy." Mike hoped the tech would come up with viable locations because he needed to be doing something. Anything to put him closer to Shelby.

"He triangulated the dump sites in relation to the concert venue. We have ten abandoned warehouses in that radius."

Mike reached out and put his hand on Daniel's shoulder. "Great job. All three of the warehouses used have been abandoned for more than a couple of years, see if he can narrow the locations down starting with the oldest. We'll hit that one first."

Daniel nodded and dialed the tech's number again.

Taking a deep breath, Mike finally moved toward Madge. He had questions for her, but he's been avoiding the look of agony on her face. He had to bury what he felt so he could think straight. doing so was the only way Shelby was getting out of this alive. "Madge," he called out as he approached.

She turned from the view of the skyline. She hadn't moved from her position in the big driveway. "My turn?"

He nodded. "I need to ask you about Robert Charleston."

His question must have surprised her. Her eyebrows puckered, and she cocked her head to the side. "He's a kid. We took him on in Nashville, and he's been a hard worker. Never complains, never even asks for a raise. He's been training with one of the lighting techs for the last six months, and he's a fast learner. What about him?"

"Did you see him today during rehearsal?"

She nodded.

"Does he room with anyone? Someone he's close to on the tour?"

She shook her head. "No. He keeps to himself and usually finds a place somewhere else to sleep. The crew talked to him about it once, but he's a little antisocial so they left him alone. He shows up on time and keeps his mouth shut."

"Has he shown any undue interest in Shelby?"

Again, she shook her head.

But he could see she was thinking about the kid in a different way. Madge hadn't come out and asked him, but she was getting there.

"No, but I've seen him give Rebecca things from time to time. No one but the band knew about her, because we'd been in Nashville for a break until we left for this tour. Then she started showing up with us to rehearsals and went on the road with us again."

"But most of your crew and the band knew Rebecca because of Abby, so her presence wouldn't have been a surprise."

"Except for Robert," Madge said, slowly. "He was brand new to the tour, and he's been doing little jobs for just about everyone."

"So he's invisible?"

"You mean to Shelby?"

Mike nodded. "Especially to Shelby. He was someone in the background, who was listening and watching but just part of the crew. I know she's close to her band, but she wouldn't be with the crew all the time, because they travel ahead and prep everything for her shows."

A look of horror crossed her face. "I was teasing Shelby about you, and he was on stage setting up a ladder just at that moment." Madge crossed her arms and hugged herself. "I never thought a thing about it. We did a background on him."

"Your people did a criminal history check on him because he was a late arrival, but the research was right before you left so the report wasn't even close to being complete."

"So why are you looking at him?"

"Robert Charleston committed suicide a long time ago. The person using his identification is the man who's been stalking Shelby and murdering women who look enough like her to fuel his twisted fantasies."

"And I hired him." The look on her face said she took all the blame. She stumbled backward.

Mike reached out and grabbed her by the arms. "Who on the crew knows him the best?"

"Probably Burt, he's the lighting supervisor, and he's been working closely with Robert the longest, teaching him the business."

"Good. Get him on the line and start asking if knows where Robert goes at night or what he does when he's not working. Anything could help. Also, what does Robert look like? We can't find a picture of him anywhere."

"He's never around for any of the crew photos. I never found that weird until now," she mused. Then she shook herself and answered, "He's average height, average weight. He's a white male with sandy brown hair and brown eyes. No remarkable features or tattoos or anything. He's just an average kid."

"Better description than we had before. Go ahead and call Burt, he might have more."

Madge pulled out her phone as Mike turned away.

He was in a holding pattern now, waiting for information, and he wanted to see for himself the blood on the balcony. The hand on his arm stopped him. Madge was back together, but just barely. He raised an eyebrow at her in question.

"Please talk to Rebecca," she begged. "She really took to you, and she knows something is wrong. No one has said anything, but she's already been through this with her mom." Her voice caught, "She won't even look at me."

Mike nodded once. He had no idea what to say to the little girl, but he'd gone through something similar. His own father had been Special Forces and was gone a lot. One day, he just never came home. Not until he himself had joined the military had he understood fully what they meant by a "training accident." That had been the official cause of death listed for his father, but the reality was that he'd been killed on duty, in a country where he shouldn't have been. The Medal of Honor Mike and his mother received a year later hadn't done anything to alleviate the despair they both felt. He'd stand at the window day after day, wishing and praying for his dad to come home, even though Mike had been told he never would.

He found Rebecca on the floor huddled in the corner of the den, surrounded by her stuffed animals. She stared off into space—no tears, no hysterics, just mute confusion and maybe a little anger. He squatted down so that he was on more of her level. "Rebecca?"

She stared straight ahead.

No acknowledgement that he was speaking. "Honey, look at me," he said. By that time, the rest of the adults had moved away to the other side of the room to give them a bit of privacy.

And still, she wouldn't budge.

"It's happening again, isn't it? Just like with your mom."

Direct hit. Her eyes widened, and she started blinking rapidly, coming out of her stupor. Turning her head, she looked up at him, her face full of questions.

He recognized she couldn't bring herself to voice them. But at least she was back in the room with him, instead of locked away inside her silent world. "And no one tells you anything. Is that right?"

She nodded and hugged a stuffed animal closer.

"She's missing, Rebecca, but she didn't leave willingly. Do you understand that?"

A slow nod, and then her voice emerged. "Bobby took her."

Mike went still, but he kept his voice low and calm. "How do you know that?"

Rebecca ducked her head and buried her nose into the soft fur of the animal in her arms. "I saw him," she whispered.

"And his name is Bobby?" When he saw her nod, he went on. "What did you see?"

"I was playing in the closet 'cause I couldn't sleep. Aunt Shelby doesn't mind, and she didn't know I was there 'cause I snuck in."

"What happened when you were in the closet?"

"Bobby was outside, and he grabbed her." Her voice was barely audible.

Mike resisted the impatience coursing through him. He didn't want to scare her. "How do you know Bobby?" Rebecca peeked up at him with her big cornflower blue eyes so much like Shelby's that his heart flipped over.

"He works with Aunt Shelby's crew and he gave me this," she said, holding out the toy she was hugging—an old-fashioned sock monkey. "He said he had dolls, too."

Her innocent comment was like an icy finger on his back. He did indeed collect dolls. Living ones that he brutalized and tortured for his own sick pleasure. Mike blocked those images and continued his questions. "What else did he say?"

"Why did he hit her?"

He couldn't take it, so he sat on the floor and pulled

Rebecca up into his lap. Rocking her back and forth, he ran his hand over her soft hair and down her back. He wished she would cry and get her feelings out. The stark containment and the way she held herself in check weren't natural for a girl her age. Or anyone for that matter. "He's not a nice man, Rebecca."

"But he's always been nice to me," she said, holding up the monkey in front of them both. "He said he'd take me to his playhouse and show me his dolls sometime, if he could get Aunt Shelby to come, too."

Shit. They'd been so focused on Shelby that none of them had even considered this bastard might have been watching Rebecca, too. After all, she was a miniature version of both her mother and Shelby Lynn. "Did he say where his playhouse was?"

"No." She fidgeted with the material on the monkey's head. "He said it was a secret place but he liked it because of the trains." She looked up into his face. "Bobby likes trains almost as much as he likes dolls."

Mike hugged her close. Their biggest clue to Shelby's whereabouts had come from the most unlikely source. Everyone knew Rebecca didn't talk. Hadn't spoken a word in over a year. Larry, a.k.a Bobby, wouldn't have known that she would begin talking again. He probably wouldn't have said anything otherwise.

"Did Bobby take my Mom too?"

"I don't know, honey. I really don't. But when I find him, it's something I will ask him, okay?"

She nodded. "I miss her."

If his heart squeezed any harder, then the pain would wreck him. This time when he hugged her, she turned and threw her arms around his neck. "I don't want Aunt Shelby to never come back."

"I'll bring her home."

She put the sock monkey into his arms, and then she climbed out of his lap. "If you give this back to Bobby, maybe he'll give Aunt Shelby back to us."

Mike nodded, choking on the lump in his throat and unable to speak. He got to his feet as well, leaned down, and kissed her on the top of the head, before turning and leaving the room. There was no way he was letting that little girl down. He had to bring back Shelby.

"Is there a reason you're choking that sock monkey to death?" Jesse asked, when Mike joined him in the foyer.

"The son of a bitch gave this thing to Rebecca at some point." He set it down on the closest table before he ripped it apart. "She was hiding in the closet when he took Shelby."

"Shit. She saw everything?"

Mike nodded. Zach came down the stairs just then. "What did you find?"

Zach glanced around, making sure they were alone.

They were, Mike had made sure to close the doors to the den behind him, so no one inside that room could hear anything. "He tried to get into the little girl's room first, but she must have been somewhere else. Then he went to Shelby's balcony. I spotted a couple of drips of blood, nothing serious, and the trail leads off the mountain to the backside where it ends. Only one set of tracks, so she was unconscious when he got her into the car."

"Rebecca wasn't in her room because she was playing in Shelby's closet," Jesse told Zach.

"How's she doing?"

Mike answered the only he could. "She's holding up the best way she knows how. But she told me something that might help. Where's Daniel?"

Jesse nodded toward the driveway. "He's out there with a map and a marker talking with that tech guy. They're narrowing down our options."

Mike headed outside toward Daniel, with Jesse and Zach flanking him. "Are any of the viable warehouses near railroad tracks? Or the actual train station?"

Daniel didn't question him, just asked the question into his phone.

They all looked at the map spread out before them.

Damon came up to the table. "The license plate was stolen from a used car lot, five blocks from the stadium. I'm guessing the car is as well. That's a dead end."

Mike nodded. He figured it might be, but he was covering every base they had. "Thanks for checking."

Daniel was talking and circling areas on the map. "Okay, great. Got it. Thanks, Lance." He hung up and pointed. "Three abandoned warehouses are near the tracks and one is next to the train yard."

"That one," Mike said. "The one next to the train yard. That's the one." If this guy liked trains then just being next to the tracks might not be enough, he'd want to be in a place where he could look at the trains any time he wanted.

No one questioned him. No orders were given. No doubts expressed.

They functioned together with a single goal.

Find Shelby.

What happened with Larry Ashbrooke when they found him, no one voiced aloud. But there was a good chance he would never see the inside of a jail cell.

CHAPTER 18

*S*helby had never considered herself one of those pathetic shrinking-violet types that faint at the first sign of trouble. But that was before she'd been kidnapped by a deranged lunatic who spent his time cutting up women.

Upon waking, she could only conclude her mind had shied so violently from a killer's touch that it had just simply shut down. The last thing she remembered was the man undressing and touching her. She flinched at the memory.

Then she realized something. Her body had moved. She'd felt that flinch.

As slowly as she could, she opened her eyes. Her head was down, and she found she was looking at her chest. *And oh Thank God*, she thought to herself. She'd been redressed in one of her concert dresses. Flame red, the gown was covered with thousands of sparkly sequins. She wasn't naked, and that seemed like a huge victory in that moment.

Shelby became aware of everything at once. Her mind was clear of whatever drug had been used, leaving her with a throbbing head and a touchy stomach. Her hands were tied on either side of her body. The rope cut into her skin. Her feet were tied together, but didn't seem to be anchored to anything. She thought she was in a chair, but didn't want to lift her head just yet to check.

And she didn't feel—used. Not that she was foolish enough to think that wasn't on the agenda at some point. Shelby just hoped Mike found her before that.

Before something worse happened.

She could hear humming in the distance, to her right. Turning her face very slightly, she saw someone lighting candles. Hundreds of them. The place was alight in the glow of so many burning wicks. Her head still throbbed, so she lifted it from where her chin rested on her chest, to ease the ache.

"I was wondering when you'd wake up. I was worried I gave you too much of the cocktail," he said.

"What did you give me?" she asked, turning to get her first look at him. And fought off the surprise. "Robert? I mean, Bobby?"

He chuckled. And it was such a sinister sound to come from such a young man. He was all of nineteen, but Shelby had seen him working with and around the crew. More recently, he'd been learning how to deal with the lighting.

"Oh come on, Shelby Lynn, don't play dumb. You knew those videos were from me."

She didn't know what to say or do. Somehow, shouting a denial and pissing him off didn't seem reasonable, but acting out a role in his fantasy didn't seem wise either. So she tried to play it safe. "Where are we?"

She looked around slowly, taking in the large space. Windows were placed up high, letting her know the sky was still dark. Small piles of crumbling drywall lay here and there, and the place had a smell she couldn't quite place, but the odor made the hair on her arms stand up. Shelby tried not to gag at the smell of blood.

Not hers.

Bobby looked around as well, following her glances. Candles were lit on shelves, on the floor, and any other surface he could find. "This is my playhouse."

Bile rose in her throat. "What do you want from me, Bobby?"

He stood in front of her, dressed in a long sleeve black shirt and matching pants. His hair was brushed back off his forehead. He smiled down at her.

The slap was unexpected and rocked her head to the side before the sting hit. The strike was on the good cheek, but the force made the bruised side burn as well.

"My name is Larry. Say it."

His voice was deeper than it had been. Odd. "L-Larry," she stammered as her eyes watered. "Why did you hit me?"

"I didn't," he said. Then he shrugged. "Charles did."

Shelby was in more trouble than she thought. The man calling himself Larry was alone with her in the room. "Who is Charles?"

"He's my cousin," he answered. Then he went over to a set of cages sitting on top of a table. "These are Romeo and Juliet."

Inside the cage were two furry little creatures. They looked like fat squirrels with runty little tails. Shelby had never seen chinchillas in person, but she knew that's what they were.

"Fitting don't you think?"

"What's fitting?"

He cocked his head and sort of hissed out, "*She knows. She's taunting you.*"

Shelby's eyes widened as the man slapped himself on the head.

"No, she doesn't. She's not like the others."

Bobby, Larry—whatever his name was—spoke in two

distinctly different voices. As if he was actually talking to someone else in the room. He didn't even seem aware of hitting himself in the head. Larry's voice was younger-sounding and matched his looks. The other voice was the stuff of nightmares.

"Larry?" She hated to draw his attention back to her, but it seemed wise to keep him talking.

He moved closer.

"I've always liked those names, but I've never seen that kind of animal before. What is it?" If she played dumb and kept asking him questions, then maybe Larry would stay with her and the other guy wouldn't reappear.

"They're chinchillas. Charles got them from a girl, but he didn't really like them so I took them. He used to tell me about them when I was in that place, and he said I could have them. They like me better. I can tell."

"I bet they do," she said. "Where is Charles now?"

"Listening," Larry whispered. "He's always butting in."

He looked around as if he expected Charles to show up around the corner or from out of a different room. His action made her glance around the space.

"I call him the Shadow Man."

"That sounds scary," she whispered back.

Larry nodded. "He can be, and he makes me do things. . ." He trailed off and looked back over his shoulder. "But I don't want to talk about that. I want to talk about us."

Shelby took a deep breath and forced a smile onto her face. "Okay."

Larry smiled back and reached out.

Shelby flinched. The movement was reflexive but she knew instantly that she'd made a terrible mistake.

His hands fisted and the smile twisted into something ugly. Even the sheen of his eyes flattened out. "*Bitch*," he hissed in the deeper voice. He had his hand in her hair, pulling it viciously and forcing her head close to his. *"Don't ever do that again. I'll touch you when and where I like. Got it?"*

Tears pooled from the pain, but she didn't let them fall. She tried to nod, but his fist only tightened in her hair. "Yes, I understand."

"I had to teach your friend how to act too," he said.

The pain was momentarily forgotten as he loosened his grip. Shelby stared upward. "What did you do with Abby?"

"Who the fuck cares? Forget about her," he said. To emphasize his point, he punched her in the stomach.

The air whooshed out in a rush and would have doubled her over if she hadn't been tied to the chair. This time, she couldn't stop the tears from falling or the cry of pain from escaping. No one had ever hit her before—not in the face, not anywhere. The pain blended with the humiliation of just taking it and being helpless to do anything. It scared her that he could beat her to death and she would just have to take it. Dear God, was this what Abby had gone through? Shelby was sick down to her soul thinking about her friend.

"Stop it, stop it, stop it," Larry said, his voice high and whiny—punctuated by a slap-slap-slap to his head. "You said you wouldn't hurt her."

"I just want to know what happened to Abby," Shelby wheezed. "Can you tell me, Larry? Please?"

Larry squatted down and pulled a snowy white handkerchief from his back pocket. He gently patted her face, removing tears and black smudges. She was confused for a moment but then realized that he must have applied makeup when he dressed her. She was glad she'd been unconscious at the time.

"He doesn't like me to tell secrets," he said. "But he knows how I feel about you, so maybe he won't mind."

"I promise not to tell him," Shelby said, making it sound like a co-conspiracy. The searing pain in her abdomen had lessened so she could talk without huffing out the words, but she was a bit worried about one of her ribs. It had taken the brunt of the punch, and didn't feel quite right.

"He hit her. Over and over again, and then she stopped breathing," he said. "I didn't want him to kill her, but then he gave her to me, and I took her to my playhouse."

Shelby held in the cry. Deep down inside, she'd known Abby was dead, but she'd held onto stubborn hope that her friend wasn't. Not just because she loved Abby, but because of Rebecca. Their precious girl didn't deserve to grow up without her mother.

He touched her arm.

Shelby was feeling so low that she didn't even notice at first.

"She was special to you, so I made sure to bury her in that special place."

Shelby nodded. "Thank you," she whispered, even though she wanted to scream or claw his face. But she didn't want his "Charles" personality to return. This young man in front of her was crazy—off his rocker, split personality, murderously insane, and anything she could do to keep him from killing her was a win. "Tell me about your videos. The ones you sent to me." She tried to smile again, but was afraid it came out more of a grimace than anything else.

He didn't seem to notice. "Did you really like them?" he asked. "Now you know why you can't quit singing. You have so many songs about us, and I want to hear more. Forever. Just you and me."

He stood again and pulled another chair over from somewhere behind her. Once he was seated in front of her, he leaned forward and caressed her face.

She was expecting his touch this time and held perfectly still. "I was only quitting because of—" she cut off. Shelby could have bitten her tongue off as nausea churned in her gut. Drawing his attention to her little girl wasn't something she'd meant to do.

"Rebecca," he finished for her. "I tried to bring her here for you, but I couldn't find her. She's so pretty, just like you. I wanted you both, but Charles wouldn't let me stay and find her."

The staggering relief she felt at his words would have driven her to her knees if she hadn't already been sitting. Thank God. No matter what happened to her, Rebecca was safe.

"Those videos were really good, Larry. Tell me how you did them," Shelby implored. She'd done so many interviews and shows during her time as a star that she could put enthusiasm into her voice easily, even when it was something distasteful.

Nothing she said mattered. She was just stalling for more time. More life.

∼

"This is the place," Daniel said, checking out the map.

Mike looked around. The site seemed right. The train yard was next door, and this was the only empty warehouse that fit the M.O., but something was off. He wasn't sure what, but his gut was telling him this place was empty and had been for some time. He hoped he was wrong.

They'd arrived in two separate vehicles. Zach and Jesse were on the north side of the building, and Mike, Daniel, and Damon were on the south side. They had state-of-the-art communication and enough weapons to take out Osama Bin Laden again. What Mike wished they had more than anything was a magic eight ball that could tell him for sure he wasn't wasting time. He didn't know what kind of time Shelby had, but whatever she was enduring until he got to her was unthinkable. "Spread out. I don't see the car, but that doesn't mean this isn't the place," Mike said softly.

"You don't sound sure," Zach stated. The sound was a whisper in Mike's ear, because Zach was somewhere on the other side of the warehouse.

"Doesn't feel right," Mike answered.

"Then let's get in and out fast, and on to the next place," Jesse said.

With that, they fell quiet. They all knew the same hand signals and thought the same way about approaching the building, so it was easy enough to fan out and take up their positions. Mike was going in first through the front, with Zach took the rear door.

Daniel had bolt cutters to snip the locks on the front, and he did it quietly. The door itself was a problem, but Damon took care of that with a can of spray lubricant. They had it open as quietly as they could manage and were inside in a matter of moments.

Switching to night-vision goggles, Mike cleared the front room fast. Damon swept right and Daniel went left, leaving Mike the door to the main area of the building. The door stood open and Mike went in cautiously. Bursting through a door could get Shelby and him killed.

Echoes of "clear" came in through his earpiece as all the rooms were checked and found empty. Mike lowered his gun at the same time Zach did as they stared at each other across the vast empty room. "Damn," Mike said.

"This was a good guess," Jesse said. "And that's what we're working with here."

"The place has got to be here somewhere," Mike said. His fists clenched and unclenched with impotent rage. He needed to get to Shelby.

"There could be newly empty spaces that we don't know about yet. Maybe something that hasn't gone on the market

185

yet?" Daniel pulled out his flashlight and studied the map again.

"Damon," Mike said. "I need you to get up high and look around for me."

"I'll hit the roof and use my scope. I'll let you know what I see in five minutes." Then he took off toward the back.

"Jesse and I will head out closer to the train yard to take a look around. I don't think this is the wrong area, just the wrong building," Zach said, putting a hand on Mike's shoulder. "We're close."

Mike nodded. "I know, man. I can feel it."

They took off, and Mike and Daniel stared at the map. An idea was taking shape, and he wanted to see the map for himself. This guy's thing was trains for some reason. What if he was in the actual train depot? That place had been empty for years since the new facility was built down towards Tucson. Eventually, all the trains would be sent there and the tracks removed to make way for new construction. "Damon," he said inside his mic. "Look to the north, toward the train yard. Jesse and Zach are headed there now."

"Shit, I should have considered that place," Daniel said. "It's perfect."

"You did. It's on the list but it's only been abandoned for about four months, and I wanted older properties," Mike said, pointing toward the bottom of the list. "Let's go." This felt like the right move. His gut was yelling at him to get there.

Daniel folded the map as they both exited the building and started north at a jog.

"Found the car," Jesse said. "It's parked next to the fence behind some overgrown hedges. He's going in and out through a hole in the fence."

"Light is coming from inside the depot. The windows are up too high for me to see anything, but something is definitely lighting up the inside," Damon confirmed.

"This is it," Zach chimed in. "I can smell blood."

Mike's stomach dropped as his friend's voices whispered through the earpiece, but he upped his pace and met Jesse by the fence. Daniel was right behind him. "Where's Zach?" he whispered.

Jesse nodded toward the shadows at the corner. "He's making his way toward the door."

"I'm joining him," Mike said.

"On my way," Damon said.

"Sit on the car, Damon. I don't want this bastard getting past us," Mike told him.

"Got it."

"Only two doors, both facing the yard," Zach said. "Jess, go around and cover any exits to the west. Daniel, go east. Make sure this guy doesn't slip past."

"I'm coming to you," Mike said.

"I didn't doubt it," Zach answered.

They split up and converged on the shadows Zach used for cover. Mike moved into position behind the big man. Daniel and Jesse were swallowed up in the inky darkness of the building.

Mike was glad Zach was there with him—if the door was locked, Zach would have it open within seconds. Zach's skill with a lock-pick was just about legendary.

"Listen," Mike said. He could hear a voice, very faintly. It echoed softly in the emptiness of the space. A row of windows along this wall faced the yard and the hulking remains of box cars not in use. Some kind of covering over the glass blocked the view, but cracks of light shown here and there. Even a caboose sat off to one side.

"They're on the other side." Mike nodded toward the door that was farther away.

"Then this is the one we want open." Zach was already on a knee with a small kit in his hands. His gun lay next to him as he pulled out a couple of slim tools and went to work.

Forty-five seconds later, Mike heard the soft snick of the lock tumbler.

"Give me two minutes and then go inside. Jess, Daniel? In position?"

"Yes," Jesse replied, followed by Daniel's affirmative a second later.

Mike kept his ear pressed to the door as he counted off the time in his head. He moved closer to a window where there was a tear he could see through.

The room was open and empty, just like the other places had been, with the exception of a few things. In the farthest corner from where Mike knelt was a bed. The covers were neatly made and candles were on the nightstand. At the door where Zach was headed was a large table with ropes tied to each leg. The ropes lying on the ground in piles were long and dark in places, probably from blood—they were restraints. He couldn't let himself think about the horror inflicted to the victims upon that table.

Several knives stood upright, their tips buried into the wood. Cleanliness was not a priority for this guy as the knives were also covered in a dark dried-on substance that was more than likely blood. The concrete floor around the legs was also covered in dried blood. A large plastic bucket sat directly under the table. Mike would bet the table had a hole in the middle and the blood from the women was drained into the bucket.

Hence, the smell.

Adjusting his position allowed him to see the rest of the

room. And Shelby. His breath hitched as he searched her face.

She was tied to a chair facing him. The left side of her face was swollen, but covered by stage make-up and she wore a red dress. Larry had stolen quite a bit from the crew before he carried out his little plan.

The man in question was seated directly in front of Shelby, caressing her face. Mike summoned herculean patience to keep himself from lunging inside and choking the life out of the bastard. What else he did in the hours that he had her, Mike didn't want to think about, because then nothing and no one would keep him from killing the man with his bare hands.

Just then the man reared back and slapped her, and Mike growled into the mic. "Now, Zach, now."

"Keep it together. One more minute, and I can give you back-up."

Larry stood so fast that the chair went flying over backward, and he stepped toward the table with the knives.

"Time's up. I'm going in," Mike said.

"Shit," was the soft reply.

Mike grabbed the door handle, wrenched it open, and stepped inside.

CHAPTER 19

"*aybe if I cut up that pretty face, you won't find my touch so repulsive,*" Charles gritted.

"I'm sorry," Shelby rasped.

He moved toward the table behind her.

If she turned her head as far as she could, Shelby could just barely see it and the knives sticking out of the surfaced. "Please don't hurt me anymore," she pleaded.

"*I haven't even begun to hurt you,*" he snarled.

"And you won't get another chance."

Mike's voice was the equivalent of angel's harps to Shelby. He was her miracle. He'd found her. The tears she'd been valiantly holding back spilled over as he stepped into the room. *Thank God.*

He was dressed in black fatigues; the gun in his hand looked enormous. And when he fired, the sound was so loud that she wished she could've covered her ears. She thought she heard a noise that sounded like s feral animal snarling, but she couldn't see anything and her ears were still ringing from the shot so she wasn't sure.

And then her head was jerked back so violently that she

worried her neck might break. Larry's breath was in her ear, and something cold and sharp was pressed under her chin. He'd grabbed a knife.

"Come any closer, and I'll slide this blade up into her brain," he said.

The hold on Shelby's head loosened, and she moved her head forward a fraction. The action was a mistake because the blade nicked the soft flesh under her chin. Warm liquid ran down her throat. More warm liquid dripped onto her mostly bare thigh, where the slit in her gown was. Maybe he cut her worse than she'd thought? Wide eyed, she stared at Mike. He was her knight in black fatigues and he would save her.

"You're already hit," Mike said. "Give up, and you don't have to die, Larry."

That must be what she felt dripping steadily onto her thigh—Larry's blood. She never thought of herself as a vengeful person, but she wanted him to hurt. The way he'd already hurt her, and the way he'd hurt those other women.

"Larry doesn't live here anymore," he growled. *"That moron weakling let me take over a long time ago."*

Shelby felt Charles moving around behind her, using her as a shield. She watched as Mike put away his gun slowly, one hand out in a "wait" gesture. "Why don't you tell me who you are then?"

A cruel laugh huffed out beside her ear, blending with the faint ringing still present. She didn't think Larry was there anymore, just his psychopathic second personality.

"You're a cop, right? One of ones guarding this bitch. Why don't you tell me who I am?"

Mike kept him talking as Zach crouched in the door

behind Shelby and Larry Ashbrooke. Zach couldn't shoot the man without the bullet ripping through Shelby. She was his shield in front and back. The only way to make sure Shelby wasn't killed was to coax out Larry to fight or keep him occupied enough so Zach could get in behind him.

Mike cocked his head to the side and stepped closer. He tried to look like he was thinking it over. "I honestly have no idea who you are. I know about Larry and his past, but nothing about you."

"*And you never will,*" he sneered. "*You might have been smart enough to find me, but that's all you'll ever do.*"

The man using Shelby as his cover was so average in every way that Mike understood how he'd seemed so unthreatening to everyone. Only now, trapped, was his true nature seeping out. The sneer on his face twisted his lips into a grotesque grin that matched the madness in his eyes. The fire that burned inside was something Mike would never understand. "Why don't you stop cowering behind the woman and come out and play with me?" He made his tone mocking. "Or can't you perform unless your victim is tied up?"

"*Maybe I'll just kill her,*" the thing using Larry's body said.

Mike shrugged. "Either way, I'll get paid, and you'll be dead." He couldn't look at Shelby and hadn't since he'd walked into the room. If he really looked at her, into her beautiful, scared face, he'd lose it and get them both killed. Mike just hoped she knew that he was doing and saying whatever he must to make sure she lived. Because a world without her was nothing to him. He'd survived all these years because she was out there. Somewhere. Her voice had come to bed with him over the years, and he'd never missed a single televised appearance.

Then she'd swept in and again taken his heart. But even that wasn't true, because she'd had it all along. He'd never stopped loving her. But right now, his job was to make sure Rebecca didn't lose another loving mother.

"*You lie. I saw you kissing her, touching her.*"

Mike had moved one more step closer, but he froze.

"*She spent all weekend fucking you, didn't she? I told Larry she was just another whore,*" he jeered. "*Stop moving.*" A gun materialized from under his shirt.

Mike tensed. He hadn't seen it because Larry's shirt was so loose. Larry's right hand held the knife under Shelby's chin, but he lowered it to her chest as he aimed the gun in his left hand. Blood flowed from the shoulder wound Mike had inflicted, but the bastard had moved so fast he'd only been winged.

Zach moved slowly and silently closer while Mike kept the maniac's attention. In slow motion, Mike saw his hand flex and his finger begin to squeeze the trigger. "Go now, Zach," he yelled then threw himself forward and to the side.

Shelby screamed and kicked her legs against the ground, sending the chair backward against Larry, knocking him off balance, as the gun fired.

Searing pain ripped into Mike's chest, stopping his forward momentum and dropping him to his knees. He didn't bother looking down, instead he looked into Shelby's eyes. Her wide gorgeous cobalt blue eyes. Movement happened behind her as Zach wrestled Larry to the ground and away from Shelby.

Jesse burst into the room during the struggle. But they were an inconsequential blur to him. Against his friends, that asshole didn't stand a chance.

"Mike," Shelby yelled, squirming in the chair.

"It's gonna be okay, Shel," he said. "You'll be okay."

Suddenly, Daniel was behind Mike and he seemed a bit touchy-feely for his tastes. "Damn it. You've been shot."

Seemed really fucking obvious to Mike, but he was too

tired all of a sudden to point it out. He just wanted to stare at Shelby a bit longer, knowing she was in one piece.

The yelling in the room got louder, and another shot went off.

Mike prepared for the pain, but it never came. And then he was looking at the ceiling. He must have fallen over, because Daniel fussed over him like a mother hen and talked on his cell phone. Mike heard the code for officer-involved shooting, and Daniel was requesting medics.

Cool hands cupped his face when he opened his eyes again.

"You better not leave me, Mike Hanson. You hear me?"

Shelby's touch and voice were just about the best things ever. Mike hadn't thought about dying, but if he did, and the last two things he felt and heard were her, then he'd go a happy man. "Everyone in the state can hear you," he replied.

"Keep him talking."

That was Zach. He was in the process of ripping open Mike's shirt. "That hurts, asshat."

Jesse chuckled and came into view from above. "Shut up. Zach is worried, and you know how he gets. He's been cussing steadily since you passed out."

"The bullet was armor piercing and drilled right through your Kevlar," Zach said.

The pain was intense as Zach moved him to get a look at the wound. The throbbing pulled Mike right out of that hazy plane he'd been surfing and put him square in the present. "Where's Larry?"

"Dead."

"Good. Now give me a gauze pad, and the three of you get the hell out of here, unless you want to do some explaining to the Phoenix Police Department." Mike could already hear the sirens in the distance.

"Just hold pressure, Shelby," Zach barked. "And don't let him move until the medics get here."

"He's not going anywhere," she said. "Thank you."

Zach leaned over and gave Shelby a kiss on the forehead. "Anytime."

"Hey," Mike complained. "Go home and kiss your own woman."

"We'll see you at the hospital." And then they were gone.

"Where's Daniel?"

Shelby held pressure with her left hand and stroked his hair with her right.

He wanted to take her into his arms and kiss her, but his body wasn't moving.

She looked over his head and nodded. "He's making more phone calls. Someone named Casey is coming here to help with the scene, and apparently half of your department is arriving now from the sounds of all the sirens."

"Are you okay? Did he hurt you bad?" She looked at him with clear eyes, free of the degradation he'd seen on the faces of rape victims.

"I'm okay, really. I'm burning this dress, but other than bruises and a massive headache, I'm fine." Shelby leaned down and put her soft lips on his in a soft kiss. "It's you I'm worried about."

"Takes more than one bullet to kill me."

"I was so scared." Tears ran down her face.

Mike couldn't stand it. With all his strength, he lifted his left arm and hugged her body close. Her lips found his and he took her mouth possessively.

"Damn it, Mike. Stop moving. You're bleeding all over the place," Daniel groused.

"Not sorry." His words slurred and his eyes went fuzzy. His eyelids slammed shut, and he heard the worried voices of Shelby and Daniel. He wanted to tell Shelby one more thing.

He wanted her to know that he loved her. Just in case. But he'd already nosedived into unconsciousness.

THE HOSPITAL CHAIR was relatively comfortable, and he'd sweet talked a nurse into bringing him a fold-up table to work at, so Daniel couldn't complain too much. Now if only his boss would wake up, he'd be a happy man.

Two days had passed since the train depot incident, and he'd been playing fast and loose with some evidence. To make matters worse, he'd enlisted Casey's help in the cover-up. That woman had given him no small rash of shit about it, but once he'd explained what happened, she'd fallen in line. The truth would have gotten both he and Mike fired, at the very least.

"Damn it."

Daniel looked up from his laptop to find Mike awake and frowning down at the IV tubes running out of his hand. "'Bout time you woke up." But he couldn't stop the grin as he stood and moved to Mike's side. He poured fresh water into a cup and added a straw. Holding it out to his friend, he said, "Drink."

"Take out the damn straw, and I will."

He wasn't sure if all people were this stubborn after being unconscious for two days or if it was just Mike, but the attitude made him laugh. "Fine." He took out the offending tube of plastic and put the cup in Mike's left hand.

He'd been shot in the right upper chest, so that arm was in a sling and taped to his chest to keep it still. His hand was shaky, but he drained the cup and held it out for more. After a second full cup of water, Mike settled back and looked around.

The room was filled with flowers, balloons, and get-well

cards from the guys in Homicide, the ladies in dispatch, and even a bouquet from the Mayor. The room smelled like a florist shop, but it was bright and cheerful.

If Daniel ever got shot again, he hoped he was treated with such love and respect.

"Shelby?"

"She and Rebecca are fine. Doctors checked her out, and she was banged up pretty good, but no broken ribs or nose."

Mike nodded and squeezed the cup in his hand.

What he was thinking, Daniel couldn't guess but he could see relief on his face.

"What about the guys?"

"Casey and I took care of the scene. All the evidence shows four people. Larry Charleston, Shelby, you, and I."

"What's the story?" he asked.

Daniel was happy to fill him in. "With the help of Lance and I, you played a very educated hunch and we went and checked it out. We didn't call for back-up, because we went together and didn't think we'd actually find anything. When we got there, we found Shelby in a life-or-death situation that didn't allow us to wait, or call in patrol."

"And Casey agreed to cover up the fact that neither of us fired our weapons, but the suspect is dead?"

Daniel shrugged. "She was a hard sell, but she wasn't willing to help take you down either, especially since she wanted that asshole dead as much as we did. Besides, he was killed with his own gun." He could feel his ears get hot, but he admitted, "The report states that after you were shot, I wrestled with the suspect and during the struggle, he was shot and killed."

Mike grinned. "Good for you. Glad you took the credit. You deserve it for everything you've done in this investigation."

The praise made him feel good. He looked up to Mike

and wanted to model his career after him. He was one of the most successful homicide detectives that Phoenix Police had ever had. It was uncanny how he solved some of the hardest crimes.

"So how bad is my injury?"

"Not as bad as it could be. Doctor said it was a good thing you had on your vest and that your pectoral muscles are so dense. They stopped the bullet from going through to your back and ripping its way out. You lost a lot of blood, that's why you've been out so long."

"Thank God for weight day," Mike said.

"Now that you're awake, Internal Affairs will want to interview you about the scene and what happened. After you eat something, we'll go over my report together."

"Sounds good."

"I'll call Zach and let him know you're finally with us again. He's been calling every two hours, and the hospital staff threatened to put him on the trespass log if he didn't comply with visiting hours."

The statement got a pained chuckle out of Mike. "I'd like to see them try."

And it was true. Daniel, Jesse, and Damon had to physically escort Zach from the building once Mike was out of surgery. They might not have succeeded if Elizabeth hadn't been there.

Daniel envied Mike. His friends were a special breed, and they stood by each other, no matter what. Zach had even gone as far as shaking Daniel's hand when they'd last met. He considered that a major achievement. "Shelby's been here as well, but they wouldn't let her in either, since she's not family—"

"How is she?" Mike said. "Besides her injuries, I mean?"

"She's been here, hoping to see you for two days, even with all her bruises. She looks terrible and great all at the same time. Tough, talented, and gorgeous. You're a lucky man."

The monitors beeped and a nurse came rushing in. "What is going on in here?" she asked, glaring at Daniel.

Then she saw that Mike was awake, and her stern frown turned into a smile. "You're awake. Let me get the doctor." She bustled back out.

Daniel had no choice but to move out of the way when several other nurses came rushing in, taking his temperature, checking his pulse and looking at the IV bag.

"We need you to step out of the room, sir."

"Hey, this isn't fair," he said over his shoulder.

The nurse pointed toward the door. "Out."

Daniel obeyed, but he'd seen the look on Mike's face when he asked about Shelby Lynn. That man was totally and completely in love with her. Daniel shook his head, wishing he had someone like that. After pulling out his phone, he called the one person he never would have thought would become a friend. When the gruff voice answered, Daniel said, "He's awake."

"Finally," Zach said. "I was starting to worry."

"Oh, you were just now starting to worry?"

"I'll call Shelby and let her know."

"Thanks, it saves me a call. I'll do what I can to get her in to see him. That prick administrator will have to get over the fact his staff all wants her autograph."

"Just make sure they take care of Mike, or I'll come down there again."

"He'll be fine."

"Well, he's a Marine."

"Damn right."

CHAPTER 20

*T*he concert of the year had been pushed back two weeks in order to let Shelby's bruised ribs heal, and for her face to look normal again.

Mike had been told she'd looked like a prize fighter until the bruising faded. They'd barely let him out of the hospital earlier that day. If they hadn't, he was having the guys break him out.

What he wanted was to be alone with her, not surrounded by thousands of screaming fans. He had to know if she was serious about quitting all this. And if he learned she wasn't, then he had to come up with another plan because losing her a second time wasn't an option.

"A packed house again," Zach said over the loud murmur of the crowd.

"The arena is always packed when she does concerts," Mike replied. "Daniel said she's leaving tomorrow. Back to Nashville."

Zach nodded. "For the funeral."

"They took longer than I thought to find Abby's body."

"That's because the city has more train stations, and they don't have a lot of detectives to spare on a cold case. They found her in a week. That's fast."

"Casey flew out to consult. She'll make the comparisons and close this case."

Then he fell silent. Casey wanted to make sure all the threads of this case were found and accounted for. He was proud of her and Daniel. They'd done an outstanding job, and he'd submitted both their names for commendations.

Mike chanced a look around and wished he hadn't. Elizabeth, Lily, and Dani glared at him from the row behind him. They were worried about him, but he couldn't take another day without seeing Shelby. His heart monitor jumped and beeped every time he'd tried to call her, and the nurses had gone militant on him and taken away his cell phone. He was to be on total rest while he recovered. The mandate was bullshit, but everyone had taken the doctor's orders to heart, even Shelby.

Thank God for the kids. Xavier and the twins were too excited to sit still, so they stood, twisting and turning to look at everything. They asked questions and talked non-stop. Mike was glad he was sitting with them. It was safer to avoid the wives. Zach was behind him, leaning forward and talking with him. Damon and Jesse were there as well, laughing and having a great time now that the danger had passed.

When the lights dimmed, the crowd went wild. She didn't have an opening act. Shelby wanted to do this on her own. He was damned proud of her. He couldn't imagine another performer going on with the show after everything she'd been through.

For two hours, Mike sat there, mesmerized and haunted by the woman on stage. Every time she changed clothes or played with the audience, she dazzled him a little more. Her voice, her songs, and her stage presence held several thousand fans in awe.

Then she walked off stage for the last time, and the crowd was on its feet. Yelling and begging for more. Always more. That was his cue.

He got to his feet and stepped out into the aisle. The microphone put into his hand was courtesy of Zach. How he'd talked the sound guys into giving him one, Mike could only guess.

"Shelby Lynn," he said. Then he repeated her name.

And the crowd went silent in confusion.

"I need a word with you." He stood in the aisle, not yet ready to be in the spotlight. This was her arena, and he wasn't comfortable with the venue, but he was determined. It had to be in this place.

And then her voice lit up the night again. "Mike?"

"I need to tell you something, Shelby Lynn."

She came back out onto the stage, gazing into the audience.

The crowd wasn't sure what to do. A smattering of applause started and stopped, and everyone looked around, trying to figure out where he was.

Shelby was out of her stage dress and stood there simply in an oversized t-shirt and blue jeans. And she was looking right at him.

A halo of bright light surrounded him from the spotlight that finally zoomed in on his position.

"What the hell are you doing out of the hospital?" she asked, one hand on her hip.

"They wouldn't let you in to see me." And that was the truth of the matter. He needed to see her, to touch her, to love her—for the rest of his life. What he needed to know now was if she was ready for that.

"Well, you got me back out here." Her voice softened. "What's your question?"

"Do you love me?"

"I wrote a song about us, Mike. The one you heard at the cabin. That was for you."

He looked up at her. Just her. No band, no back-up singers. Just Shelby. Standing up on stage talking to him as if thousands of people weren't listening.

"I've written all my love songs about this man," she said to the audience with a wave of her arm. "You see, I've loved him since I was a teenager, but I broke his heart when I left him to follow my dream."

The women in the crowd all sighed at once.

Mike couldn't move, because he was caught up in her too. In her story, in the intimate way she drew everyone in on her secret.

Then she looked at him. "The question I have is, do you still love me?"

Mike was ready and so were his friends, because he'd planned this with them. He might land flat on his ass, but he didn't care. He took three big strides and stepped into the stirruped hands of his best friends. They catapulted him upward to the stage, grinning and laughing as they did it. And even with one arm strapped to his body, he reached it.

The audience gasped and started clapping.

Mike didn't waste any time in triumph, he went to his woman. He had one useful arm and he put it to work, pulling her into him and kissing her with all the love inside of him. When he could pull away, he said, "I've loved you almost my entire life. No sense stopping now."

Tears gathered in Shelby's eyes as he got down on one knee in front of God and several thousand strangers. After pulling the velvet box out of his sling, he handed it to her.

"Marry me," he said. "Let me love you for the rest of our lives."

~

SHELBY STOOD there in awe of the man in front of her. Battered and bruised, he'd come for her. She'd been prepared to fight for him, but he was here and fighting just as hard for her. How could she not love him?

The crowd was going wild, but she'd tuned it out.

"Say yes," he said in a raspy voice.

The crowd had fallen silent.

She had no doubt their images were up on the big screen for the whole audience to see. "Do you have to do everything in front of a crowd?" she teased.

"Say yes, damn it," he growled.

His face was a mask but she could see the love shining out of his eyes. She reached down to cup his face with her hands, and he leaned into her touch. She turned and lifted the microphone to her lips. "I gave myself to all of you," she said to her fans, "but now it's time to stop and take something for myself. This is my last concert, and I hope it was my best because I love you all. You've given me an amazing life and for that, I can never thank you enough. I love this man more, and I want to be everything to him now."

Clapping and wolf whistles filled the auditorium.

"I never asked you to walk away from your music," he said. "From being a star."

"And I would never ask you to stop risking your life as a police officer. This is *my* choice, and I want this."

"Are you sure? Because I won't let you go again. I can't," he whispered.

"Say yes." Rebecca's sweet voice blared out over the loud

speakers. She stood on stage with Madge who had tears streaming down her face. "I want to live with Cinnamon."

Shelby could feel her face heat as she turned back to see Mike's face. "I might have told her that we'd live with you."

"Pretty confident, huh?"

She shook her head. "Hopeful."

"Marry me, Shelby," he said.

"Yes."

The crowd went berserk, cheering and screaming. But that all faded as Mike kissed her again, taking his time and not caring in the least that everyone was watching.

"I love you," she said.

"I know."

Shelby opened the velvet box and sucked in a breath. The ring was simple, yet stunning, just like the man who'd given it to her. "This is beautiful," she whispered.

"Put it on, Shel."

He looked down at his sling as if he wanted to rip it off and put the ring on himself, and knowing Mike, he did. But there was no way she was going to stand by and watch that, so she plucked the ring out of the velvet and slid it on.

"Now show the damn audience that you're mine."

He was finally smiling and she couldn't help but throw her head back and laugh. "Yes, sir." Shelby flashed the ring toward the closest cameraman who put her hand on the big screen for everyone to see.

Mike pulled her close and stood by her side while the crowd cheered. "I love you, Shelby Lynn."

"Just Shelby. Shelby Lynn is done. I only want to be called Mrs. Hanson now," she said.

"How about Mom?"

Shelby grinned and nodded. "Or that." Reaching up, she stood on tip-toes to kiss him and wrapped her arms around his neck. "Let's get out of here and start practicing."

"Hell yes," he said.

Rebecca was waiting for them and ran right into Mike's arms when he squatted down for her just off the main stage. She kissed him on the cheek, and he hugged her close.

Shelby's heart was full. She was starting a new chapter in her life, and she couldn't imagine anything more fulfilling than loving this man and raising Rebecca. And if they had more kids along the way, then her life would be complete. No more secrets, no more loneliness. Just love and joy.

They both deserved that happiness.

ALSO BY KORI DAVID

In Zach's Arms (Once a Marine, Always a Marine - Book 1)

Lily's Outlaw (Once a Marine, Always a Marine - Book 2

Finding Dani (Once a Marine, Always a Marine - Book 3)

www.ingramcontent.com/pod-product-compliance
Lightning Source LLC
Chambersburg PA
CBHW032124170626
46808CB00006B/2095